MR. AND MRS. SHIFT

SEMI-COZY PARANORMAL FUN

WITCHIN' IMPOSSIBLE MYSTERIES
BOOK 4

RENEE GEORGE

BARKSIDE OF THE MOON PRESS

For Steve

Thank you for loving me, even when I don't make it easy.

ACKNOWLEDGMENTS

A special THANK YOU to the fabulous Robyn Peterman, an awesomely funny writer and my favorite cookie, for allowing me the privilege to write in her world and then turning around and allowing me to turn this series into my own world. I love your guts, woman!!

Also, I must thank my BFF and critique partner Michele Bardsley. You complete me! And to my sister Robbin, whom I would be completely lost without.

To my Rebels, you all RAWK! You keep me going every day with your support. I love you to the moon and back.

To my fans, I would not be anything without you. Seriously. If you keep reading, I'll keep writing! Thank you. Thank you. Thank you. If I were reviewing you all, you would get five-gazillion stars and a million-gazillion smooches.

Oh! And lest I forget, thank you strong, black coffee. Without you, I couldn't get out of bed in the morning, let alone write a single word.

A witchy bride. An itchy groom. A flower girl squirrel. And a dead wedding planner. Why is nothing ever easy in Paradise Falls?

I'm finally marrying the love of my life, werebear Ford Baylor, in a ceremony that will bind our souls forever. But of course, party crashers have other plans for this anxious bride—like killing me before the ceremony.

With the help of Tizzy the squirrel and Lily Mason, Ford and I are determined to track down the killer and make the midnight deadline. But if we can't stop the person behind the bounty on my head, the wedding may be off. Permanently.

What's this Witchzilla to do when everything on her special day goes wrong? I do everything I can to ensure I don't lose my one shot at true happiness.

For me and the gang, it's just another day in Paradise Falls.

CHAPTER 1

"WELL, that's it. The wedding is off," chirped Tizzy, my familiar, a red flying squirrel with a flair for the dramatic. Although, in this case, there was a reason for the drama.

"The wedding is not off," I whispered harshly.

"Hazel, you no longer have a wedding planner!"

"I don't need a wedding planner," I countered. "Especially one who just tried to kill me, for Goddess' sake. Now, help me hide the body."

I manufactured a calm demeanor. Which was difficult. My wedding planner, Vivi Lashay, a perky and enthusiastic witch who had been my confidant and closest ally in my war on flowers and cake, had just tried to shoot me with a silenced Walther PK380. That was the weapon of an assassin, not a person who specialized in making brides feel special.

"Goddess, Haze," said my BFF since kindergarten, Lily Mason. She leaned over, holding her long auburn hair back with one hand so the silky strands wouldn't fall into the corpse. "Smells remarkably like barbeque mixed with ozone."

"Ewww." Tizzy skittered up to my shoulder. "You cooked her."

I gagged but managed to get it under control before dry heaves started. I had a very active gag reflex, a fact that could make some things in the bedroom more difficult, but I'd learned how to control it somewhat during my fifteen years at the FBI working serial killings and murders—and let's not forget Peter the Prick, the only flasher to ever make the FBI's most-wanted list. Trust me. He deserved prison time for waggling that diseased-pocked penis at unsuspecting women. However, Lily was right. Vivi smelled decidedly charbroiled.

Well, that was that. I'd never eat barbecue again.

Gak! I put my fingers against my lips.

"Are you going to puke?" asked Tizzy.

"No. And don't say puke." I swallowed my gorge. "Okay. The sendoff party is in a couple of hours." I tugged the hem of my slip over my knees, side-stepped Vivi's body, and used my toe to nudge the gun out of her lifeless hand.

Lily shook her head. "I heard the last time someone

did the bonding ceremony out here, the bride got hit by lightning. It might just be the place. Bad luck and all."

Bindings were a rarity, and I hadn't heard of any ceremonies taking place since I'd taken over as chief of police. "When did this happen?"

"A long time ago. Like when we were kids. It wasn't anyone my parents knew, so I could be remembering wrong. Still. Maybe we should cancel the binding or at least postpone it."

"No!" I said emphatically. "I am not canceling. I am not canceling anything." In Paradise Falls, the town is half witches, half shifters. Shifters mated for life, while witches were more like humans, in that marriages didn't always last. The founders, in their wisdom, put a halt to fly-by-night nuptials by creating a bonding spell that prevented witches from breaking their vows. The ceremony would take place at midnight tonight under the Goddess' Light Temple, aka an open gazebo on the lake. The sendoff would end at ten o'clock, and I would return to the room to change into my wedding gown and receive blessings from all the female guests before they followed me out to the gazebo to meet Ford and take his soul to mine.

Then we would be genuinely mated and wed by both witch and shifter standards. Breaking the bonds required some dark and deadly magic. I knew that for a fact. After all, my father had obliterated my mom when he'd separated his life force from hers.

Don't worry. She had it coming.

Even so, Dad had spent seventeen years in witch jail for the crime. Since Dad and Mom's break-up via explosive magic, the bonding ceremony had become optional. But since Ford didn't have a choice in loving me for the rest of his life, I wasn't going to be any less committed. I would happily join my soul to his over and over again, but that meant we needed witnesses. The binding fed off physical energy, so the more witnesses, the stronger the binding, and I'd opened the invitation to my witchy wedded bliss to everyone I could think of. I wasn't sure if I could get this many people to show up twice.

"No," I said again. "No postponement. We have twenty-eight RSVPs arriving for dinner and close to two hundred more for the binding ceremony, including some family from out of town, and I'm not going to turn them all away because of one itty-bitty, well-deserved death." I'm pretty sure I sounded hysterical, but I didn't care. I'd been planning for this week since November, and I could see my whole wedding going the way of Vivi Lashay.

Tiz, from my shoulder, looked down at the cooked wedding planner and whistled. "Goddess in a tutu, Haze. You burned a hole clean through her."

A tunnel the width of a softball had replaced the area where Vivi's heart used to be located. It had created a passage, cauterizing her flesh, arteries, and veins as it traveled through her body. I frowned. "I didn't mean to." My witch powers had been getting stronger over the past year and a half, ever since I'd come back home, but my ability to control them hadn't progressed as fast. The results were sometimes disastrous. "I only meant to shock her."

"That's not shocked." Tizzy pressed her tiny fingers to her chest. "I'm shocked." She pointed at the corpse. "That's a full-scale electrocution. The only thing missing is the electric chair."

"If she hadn't tried to shoot me, I wouldn't have had to defend myself." I walked to the window and stared out at the wedding guests milling around the yard. I was feeling shaky from the near-death experience. "Barbecued assassin is the last thing I need right now."

Lily joined me and put her arm around my shoulders. "Nobody needs this kind of thing, honey. Especially when you're trying to marry your soul mate. Even so, I'm wondering if maybe I shouldn't have your father translocate Parker back to Moonrise and wipe his memory of Paradise Falls."

I watched Lily's human boyfriend, Parker Knowles, having a conversation with my soon-to-be father-in-law. Parker laughed at something Brent Baylor said, and Brent smiled, which, in turn, made me smile. Parker had known that Lily was a cougar shifter for almost a year now, and it hadn't mattered. Lily waved to Parker from the window. He smiled up at her and waved back. He loved her. Even a blind witch could see just how much.

I patted my best friend's hand. "We are back on the Happiness Train as of now, so Parker stays. You two are adorable together, and he seems to be handling the whole supernatural town thing pretty well."

"On account of he hasn't seen the dead girl," she said. She sighed wistfully. "What if I can't protect him? You know, if the florist tries to stab you or something, and you go nuclear."

"It'll be fine." I hoped. I wish I knew why Vivian had tried to shoot me. The short time I'd been back home, I had made a few enemies. The witches who had supported Adele Adams, and the families of Jenny Weaver and Romy Quinn. Plus, I was pretty sure the High Clowder would love to see me taken down a peg or two. Even so, I didn't think any of them would hire an assassin to take me out. I know it was selfish, but I couldn't help but wish Vivi had at least waited until the reception to take me out. Now, I had to do all the wedding coordination without any professional help.

A sharp knock at the door made me yelp.

"Everything okay in there?" My father, Kent Kinsey, was doing the traditional dad thing and giving me away. This antiquated ritual based on the idea that I was somehow property to be given away made my dad happy. I liked seeing him happy. Even if it sometimes grossed me out.

For example, he and his plus one—*yuck*—were staying in the Celestial Suite, across from the Groom's Room and next to the Bride's. Which meant, we shared a wall. I had warned him that I better not hear any monkey-rooster noises coming from that direction or else. Or else what? I had no idea, but I'd make sure it wasn't pretty. What I didn't take into consideration was that he could hear noises coming from my room as well. I had apologized more than once at breakfast for scarring him for life.

"It's fine," I lied. "Everything is A-okay."

Lily said in a hushed voice, "Maybe we should just tell him. He might be able to help."

I shook my head.

"I heard shouting," Dad said.

I looked at Lily for help with a good lie. She shrugged. Absolutely no help at all. I rolled my eyes at her. She stuck out her tongue.

"Real mature," I whispered.

She grinned.

With no input from the peanut gallery, I turned to

the door and said to my dad, "It's a new stress-release technique called Scream Your Pain."

"Are you sure it's not called Getting Cold Feet?" he asked.

"No!" As if. There was nothing cold about my feet or my feelings for Ford Baylor.

"Can I come in?"

"No!" shouted Tizzy, Lily, and I at the same time.

My father had a penchant for translocating into a room on a dime, so I added, "I'm naked."

"All right. I'll check on you in a bit."

"Thanks, Dad." I gave Tizzy side-eye. "Find me a place to put Vivi until I can think of something better. People are going to be traipsing in and out of this room for an hour before the ceremony, and I can't have them tripping over her corpse."

"Why don't you just use your magic and store her somewhere private, I don't know, like say, Wyoming, until after the festivities," Lily said.

"My magic is unpredictable when I'm feeling calm. When I'm not calm," I gestured to the body, "I blow holes in people. Knowing my luck, I'd shoot for Wyoming and end up with an inside-out Vivi on my cake table."

"Fair point," Lily said. "Nothing ruins a good wedding ceremony like corpse cake-topper."

Tizzy sighed. "You know, hiding a body is very uncop-like behavior." She affected disappointment. "You're the chief of police. This could seriously affect your reelection."

I shooed her off my shoulder. "It won't matter if someone murders me."

Tizzy tugged my hair. "Now who's being dramatic."

"You weren't here when she pointed that gun at me. Trust me, no extra drama here." I glanced at Lily. "I think you better find Ford."

Tizzy sighed theatrically. "Do we really have to involve old furry, saggy butt?"

"He has a middle-aged, sexy, firm-as-hell butt, and no fur on it, at least not when he's in his human form."

"Is this really the best topic of conversation considering the…" Tizzy gestured to the body.

"You think she cares?" I looked at Lily. "Will you get Ford for me?"

"Of course," she said.

The high-pitched voice of doom said, "Isn't it bad luck to see the bride before the wedding?"

"Don't be daft. Besides, I don't think my luck can get any worse."

Lily flinched. "Did you really have to say that? It's like inviting the Bad Luck demons to up the ante."

"Death by electric zap is gonna be hard to top." Tizzy jumped off my shoulder, spread her arms and legs, and glided to the vanity. Her soft, proficient landing would have given Superman a run for his money. She gave me a final look of disdain. "All I have to do is find a hiding spot for a dead wedding planner in a farmhouse full of people. Nooo problem."

Lily squeezed my hand. She walked to the door and opened it a crack. "I'll be right back with Ford."

"Don't you mean Fuzzy Wuzzy," Tiz corrected and slid through the opening.

"Please don't call—"

Tizzy was gone before I could finish.

Lily looked sympathetic. "I can talk to her if you want. I think she's just scared."

"Of what? I think I've proven I'll go to great lengths to not lose her." I'd even given up being a witch, which royally blew, for a short period of time when the High Clowder—which is just a formal way of saying a familiar council made up of a bunch of stuck-up cats—had tried to take her away from me and assign me some hairless nimrod named Lonnie in her stead. When I refused, they stripped me of my magic.

Let me just say here and now, being human, even for a couple of days, sucked ginormous, non-magical, hairy balls.

"I was willing to give up everything that makes me who I am to save Tiz."

"She knows that on an intellectual level, but

emotionally... She's always been the most important being in your life until you moved back to Paradise Falls. Even though you and Ford are already mates, making it official with this binding will make it official with Tizzy that she has to share you for the rest of your long, long life."

I hoped it was a long life. I almost died fifteen minutes ago, and the day wasn't over yet. "She's got a girlfriend, Lils."

"Who you dislike for the same reasons she doesn't always like Ford."

"In my defense, the cat hated me long before I hated her." But I had to admit that occasionally it hurt when Tiz would blow me off to spend time with Loopydoopy.

Lily laughed. Surprising, considering our current circumstance. "True story."

I huffed. "I'll talk to her."

"I'll be right back with your beau."

After Lily left, I got up and shuffled to the window. I sniffled. As tears streamed my cheeks, the mineral mask on my face loosened and made the clay all gloopy. Damn it. This couldn't be happening. Not on my wedding eve.

CHAPTER 2

L'AMORE CELESTIAL Gardens was a palatial three-story farmhouse on fifteen acres near Paradise Park, and the premiere venue for weddings and proms in Paradise Falls. Okay, it was the only venue. The Bride's Boudoir was a circular room with large windows located on the third floor. It had a four-poster bed near the north windows, a large vanity, a tri-fold mirror, a plush sitting area with a love seat and two overstuffed loungers, and a circular ottoman. The entire color scheme was cream and ivory, even down to the fresh flowers in large vases strategically, yet tastefully placed. It was a bride's fantasy come true.

Except for the dead body.

I would have screamed my frustration, but I didn't want my dad or his date—*gag*—charging headlong into the room. This weekend was supposed to be magical, not homicidal.

A knock at the door startled me.

The deep baritone voice on the other side said, "Haze, I'm coming in."

My stomach dipped as the scent of cinnamon rolls and pumpkin bread preceded all six feet, nine inches of hunky bear shifter. Ford opened the door wider to get his large body through, stooped under the arch, and walked inside. Goddess, he was it for me. I'd known it since my junior year of high school, and now, all those times I'd practiced writing Mrs. Haze Baylor on my notebooks would finally pay off.

The pleasant aroma of cinnamon rolls and chai lattes filled the room, overtaking the scent of charred meat. Ford's blue eyes twinkled when his gaze met mine. "Nice look," he said.

Ack. I forgot about the clay mask on my face and my hair up in curlers. "I hate that you have to see me like this on our wedding day, but we have bigger problems than my appearance."

He raised his brow. "I can see that." He closed the door behind him. "So why is Vivi Lashay on the floor with a hole in her chest?" He sniffed. "And why does it smell like barbecue?"

I pointed to the gun near Vivi without even the slightest guilt. "She started it."

"A Walther PK380, huh?" He stooped down and picked up the weapon. "That's some serious hardware."

"Right? She freaked me out when she yanked it from her purse. After she made it clear she planned to blow my brains out, I just reacted." I held up my hands and wiggled my fingers.

Ford stepped out of the direct line of my hands. "I can see that."

"The gun isn't even the worst part."

"I'd agree." He crouched down and poked his fingers into the empty space where Vivi's heart used to be.

"Don't be mean." I smacked at Ford.

He raised a brow at me. "Better her than you."

"Damn skippy." I crossed my arms. "When she was threatening me, she said there was a bounty on my head, and she'd get paid double for killing before the final binding ceremony. A bounty! That means Vivi was just the first. Why would someone rather see me dead than wed?"

His spicy fragrance grew thick and pungent. Ford's forehead wrinkled as he narrowed his eyes. "Not going to happen." He stepped over the body with one long stride and swept me into his arms. "Whatever it takes, we're getting married. We can run away right now if you want and go to some justice of the peace."

I clasped my hands behind his neck. "That doesn't have the same permanent commitment that a binding has, and I want to make sure that there is no misunderstanding that you will be mine until death do us part." I just hoped death didn't part us before the binding. "Besides, your mom would end up collecting the bounty if we tried to bail."

Bryant and Nita Baylor had shelled out a lot of dough for the L'Amore Celestial Farms venue. The cost, including the dinner tonight, had been in the six-thousand-dollar range. More money than I would have spent on a wedding, but she hadn't taken no for an answer. To anything.

"I've waited eighteen years to marry you, Hazel Marie Kinsey. I'm going to marry you tonight, and I'm not going to let anyone stop me."

"Agreed," I told my bearman. "But the only way that's going to happen is if we figure out who is behind the hit and get him or her to call it off in time for our nuptials."

The door opened and closed as Lily and Tizzy made a quick entrance.

"What took you both so long?"

"After I found Ford and sent him up, I helped Tiz look for a place to hide the body," Lily said.

"And we found one," Tizzy grumbled. "Just in case you were wondering."

"Where?" I asked.

"You're not going to like it."

"Where?"

"Under the east staircase. There's a small room, like the one where the boy wizard with the lightning bolt scar lived."

Harry Potter reference aside, private access to the staircase would be next to impossible. "We'd have to pass all the rooms on this floor, the parlor, and library on the second floor, along with the room Ford's parents are staying in." Lily was on the second floor, as well. "And even if we manage to get Vivi to the staircase unseen, there is still the crowded foyer where the base of the staircase is located."

"I told you that you wouldn't like it."

"We should ask your dad for help. He can use a translocation spell." Lily cast me a sympathetic look. "Kent is really good at those." My dad had been the one to pop down to Lily's new home in Missouri and bring her and her date back for the weekend.

"And accurate," Tizzy added. "Unlike a certain witch in the room."

"What are we going to do when more murderers come after me?"

"Easy-peasy." Ford hugged me tighter, and my knees wobbled. "They all end up in the cupboard with Vivi."

"Where do we even start with suspects?"

"The photographer, caterer, cake decorator, florist," Lily suggested. "And half the guests."

"What about the high priestess?" I asked.

Ford stroked my back. "You think Sister Sandy is behind this?"

"No." I sighed. "Not really." I just hated her holier-than-thou attitude. As if she were somehow closer to the Goddess because she had a fancy title. "It could be a guest. I'm not always the most popular witch in town. And it's not like I know everyone personally."

"Someone hiring a killer to take you out sounds pretty damn personal," Lily said.

Ford shook his head. "It doesn't mean the person paying to kill Hazel is at the wedding. So, the assassins themselves are probably just looking for a paycheck."

"I don't find that comforting," I told him. "Like, not at all." People who killed for personal reasons tended to get sloppy. Sloppy was easier to catch. Assassins were cold-blooded killers who would plan your wedding one moment and shoot you the next.

"What about all of your relatives coming out of the woodwork? You don't know those people," Tizzy said. "What if one has it out for you? Or is getting revenge for something your mom did?"

Ugh. I hated thinking about my mom. She'd been a bad seed, part of a group of power-hungry witches and shifters, and she had been responsible for the deaths of Lily's parents. My dad had accidentally blown her up when I was eighteen, and he'd spent seventeen years in confinement for it.

"That's not completely impossible," Lily agreed. "You should ask your dad about old enemies."

I pouted because I was the bride, and brides were allowed to pout on their wedding days. "Why are you trying so hard to get my dad involved?"

"Maybe because I think it's nice you have a dad to *get* involved."

My heart sank. Lily had lost both her parents and her only sibling. I imagined she would've loved to be able to ask her dad for anything. "I'll think about it." Oh, who was I kidding? I had to ask him. If someone was here to exact revenge for Mom's past misdeeds, I could be in serious trouble. She'd tangled with some pretty powerful witches and messed with forces she had no business messing with—druidic power and death magic, for example. I'd almost lost Lily because of the dark path my mom had walked.

Ford's phone beeped. He looked down at the screen. "It's my mom. She's freaking out about something. I better go check on her."

"Before you go, kiss me." I patted his cheeks. "I'm going to need something to hold me together."

"Anything for my beautiful bride-to-be." He feathered his lips over mine. I tried to deepen the kiss, but my face cracked. Ack! I still had clay on my face. "Lily, can you get me a warm washcloth?"

"Even with a mint-green face, you are sexy as hell, Haze." Ford reached down to caress my bootie. "Mmm, vanilla and rum. I love the way you smell."

"Oh yeah? And what if I smelled like cheap beer?" I reached my hand up, my fingers tracing the scruff of his short beard.

"You could smell like a raccoon's pee, and I'd still find you sexy."

"Ew." I giggled. "I'm not sure that's a smell you'd want to live with forever." I'd drunkenly kissed Ford at a party our senior year, and he'd caught my scent. The mating scent. I got the better end of the aroma stick because my man always smells like cinnamon desserts. You know, streusel, cinnamon buns, spice cakes, apple pie, and such. I'm just lucky that I'm a witch with the metabolism of a rabbit on crack. Otherwise, I'd have put on fifty pounds in the past year since returning to Paradise Falls.

I untangled from Ford and watched his firm, round ass while he walked away.

After he left, I sighed. Heavily. "What a view."

Tizzy made a noise of disgust. "I could have gone all night without watching you two grope."

"Here you go," Lily said and handed me a steaming

washcloth. "Maybe we should get the rollers out of your hair. Or at least wrap them up." She was being such an excellent maid of honor.

"I've missed you." I took the cloth and wiped the crusted clay from my face. "But my hair hasn't set yet, so the curlers stay in.

"Hazel, you cannot go out there with rollers in your hair!" Tizzy protested. "Rollers, I might add, that would be completely unnecessary if you would just practice a little glamour magic."

"Hush," I told the squirrel. "My magic is unpredictable, and I am not risking all my hair falling out on my special day."

Lily looked meaningfully at the door where my father had been pacing on the other side. "Well, there are several hundred witches and warlocks in this town. I'm sure you could have gotten someone to fix you up."

"I'm not asking my dad to fix my hair and makeup." I didn't even really need the mask, but I liked the way it made my skin tingle.

"Why wouldn't you ask your dad?" my dad asked from right behind me, nearly sending me into a full-blown heart attack.

"Mr. Kinsey," Lily said. "Nice of you to pop in."

My father looked handsome in his black suit. With his black hair and deep brown eyes much like mine, the sky-blue shirt under the jacket almost seemed ethereal. He gave me a curious look. "What are you being so secretive about?"

His question meant he hadn't noticed the body on the floor. Lily and I parted, leaving a clear path to the deceased.

My dad opened his mouth to say something. Then closed it. Then opened it. Finally, he said, "That's unexpected."

"You're telling me." I snorted inappropriately. I couldn't help it. High stress triggered my funny bone, and frankly, it didn't get much higher stress than barbecued Vivi. "She pulled a gun on me."

"What did you do?"

"I blew a hole in her. Duh."

"No, I mean, what did you do to Vivi to make her pull a gun on you? You've been riding her pretty hard these past weeks. Bridezilla is a real phenomenon."

"Dad!"

"Kidding, pumpkin." He waved a well-manicured hand. "Just trying not to lose it here."

Apparently, high-stress funny bones ran in the family. "We need to hide the body until we can find out who sent Vivi to kill me and why. I don't want the culprit knowing she's failed and initiating Plan B."

My dad smoothed his perfectly coiffed hair back with a shaky hand. He was definitely ruffled. "Plan B?"

"Sending more hired guns after me." I told him about Vivi's last words before I defended myself. "I really just meant to incapacitate her," I concluded.

"You definitely managed that and then some." He balled his fists onto his hips and shook his head. "We need to get Tanya involved."

"Noooooooo," I whined. Tanya Flipping Gellar, the town medical examiner—and my dad's new girlfriend —was also my frenemy. Friendly enemies. I didn't hate her as much as I used to, not that I'd admit it out loud. She'd had a crush on Ford before I came back to town, and the redheaded witch liked to throw shade at me left and right. "I think the fewer people involved, the better."

"When the Grand Inquisitor's special police get wind of this, and they will, you will want a forensic accounting of what occurred here. Believe me, witch prison isn't a nice place to visit, and you certainly don't want to live there. Especially not behind bars. Witch jail is not fun, Kitten. Take it from your old man."

My dad would know. He'd spent all of my adult life in a magic-free jail cell. He was also right about his mother's special police. I used magic to kill someone. Not for the first time, but it was the first time I'd used it to defend myself against a mundane weapon. Had I had my own pistol, I might have chosen that option, but at the time, all I had was my spark. I hadn't meant for it to go so high voltage. Surely, the Grand Inquisitor would cut me some slack for the innocent mistake; after all, we were family, although it hadn't stopped her from throwing my dad in jail.

I snorted again. Tizzy, Lily, and my dad all looked at me as if I were losing my mind. I sighed. "I don't want to go to the pokey. For any reason."

"Then we need Tanya."

I groaned. "But she doesn't like me. What if she uses this as an opportunity to get rid of me?"

Dad added, "She won't do anything to harm you, Haze."

"How can you be so sure?"

"Because she's going to be your stepmother."

The room, along with my mood, darkened. I'd gotten used to Tanya and my dad getting all loved up, but married? I wasn't sure I'd ever get comfortable with that notion. "I didn't think this day could get any worse."

My dad's brows dipped as he narrowed his disappointed gaze on me. "Now, Haze. Don't be that way. Tanya makes me happy."

He was right. I'd never seen him this happy with Mom when I was growing up, and I didn't have to live his life, thankfully. But it was still too much for me to handle at the moment. "I know, Dad. But I can't hear this right now. Not today. We'll make a plan to discuss it when I get back from my honeymoon."

"If you survive to the honeymoon," Tizzy said with alarming seriousness.

"I'll be fine, Tizzy." I looked at Dad and sighed. "I guess you better go get Tanya before Vivi goes into rigor mortis."

Dad vanished immediately. I really admired his ability to control translocation. Right then, I wished I could translocate Ford and me to a deserted island where no one would find us. He could hunt and gather, I could cook and... Oh, who was I kidding? Ford would end up doing the hunting, the gathering, the cooking, and the cleaning. The domestic gene was recessive in my family.

A loud squawk startled me. I turned to Tizzy, who had her perfectly manicured hand over her mouth while her whole body shook with laughter. She laughed so hard she began to wheeze. Her bushy chest heaved with the effort to breathe. I glared. She laughed harder.

Lily, like a good BFF, did not even crack a smile.

When Tizzy's hysteria ended, she wiped the tears from her rounded cheeks and said, "Hazel's getting a new mommy."

I threw the wet washcloth covered with mud at

Tizzy, but she jumped out of the way before it hit her. "My dad is never going to marry—"

A whirl of black and red tornado-ed into the room. Who wore black to a wedding? Tanya Freaking Gellar, that's who. The witch put her hands on her hips, stared down at the body with disapproval, and asked, "What kind of mess have you gotten yourself into this time, Hazel?"

CHAPTER 3

TWO HOURS and several lectures later, the body was under the cupboard, I was dressed in a metallic midnight-blue strapless Herve Leger form-fitting bandage dress, with perfectly curled hair and makeup awesome, courtesy of my dad. Thankfully, Tanya had promised not to turn me into the witch police. At least not yet. It was six-thirty, one hour before the dinner. Guests would be seated at seven, and the meal served at seven-thirty. Momma Baylor had spent a month with the caterer crafting tonight's menu, and I didn't want all of her efforts going to waste because of an attempted bridal-cide.

I texted Ford to escort me downstairs for pre-dinner cocktails. It would be the perfect time to scope out the guests and see if anyone acted suspiciously.

He texted back. **Busy.**

Get unbusy. Need my man.

Do you know someone named Carly?

Fu-udge. Not my cousin Carly. Well, she wasn't my real cousin, but she'd stayed with my mom's first cousin in a foster-like situation for a summer when I was a teenager, so I claimed her as a cousin. Barely. She hadn't RSVPed my obligatory invite. Talk about adding gas to the fire. If that crazy witch was here, we had more problems on our hands than an assassin.

On my way. I glanced at Lily then texted Ford again. **Keep Parker out of harm's way.**

Will Carly hurt him?

Probably not, but she might molest him. On second thought, distracting Carly from the man candy was perhaps a bigger job than my boo-bear could handle on his own. Hell, it might be a bigger job than I could manage. **See you in a minute.**

Or however long it would take me to venture down the steep staircase in my four-inch Jimmy Choos. If I got super lucky, I might break my neck on the way down, and I could avoid the hurricane otherwise known as Carly.

The murmur of many voices echoed up the ancient stairwell. My chest tightened with every step.

"And so, I was like, poop on a stick, and black snakes were freaking everywhere!" The garishly booming voice was followed by riotous laughter. Crap. Carly.

I hastened my pace down the last flight. I had to save my poor mate! Carly, while not evil, could be unpredictably violent. She'd been kicked out of several foster homes for blowing up garages. Once, she even exploded a car. I couldn't take the chance she'd turn my dreamboat into the *Titanic*.

I tripped down the last three steps and into the arms of a man I didn't recognize. He set me on my feet and said, "First day with new feet?"

I wiggled my scrunched-up toes and tried not to be jealous of the fact that the men had on flats while I wore spikes of doom. "Just purchased them yesterday," I said. "I haven't had a chance to break in the toes yet."

He grinned. "Are you okay?"

"Fine, thanks. I don't believe we've met," I said, working to keep the suspicion from my tone. "Are you one of Ford's friends?"

"I'm here for the bride's side," he replied. Before he could say more, I was swept up into a whirlwind known as Carly Rogers.

"Well, spank me blue and call me Nancy if it isn't my favorite cuz!" Carly squealed in my direction. Her pert boobs were on display in an extremely tight, vintage Christian Dior knock-off. She grasped me into a quick hug, tearing me away from my rescuer. "I've just been amusing myself with this big, strapping hunka man of yours."

"Yes, he is mine." I gave my guy a look of pure possession. He gave me a pleased grin. The animal in him loved it when I got territorial. "He's totally strapping."

Carly nudged me. "You got yourself a real stud." She swung an enormous purse over her shoulder and added, "Congratulations on finding such a beefcake, Haze."

"I'm surprised to see you here, Carly."

"I was invited," she said. "That's all I needed."

Ugh. I hadn't kept in touch with Carly since we were kids, so her appearance at my wedding was definitely out of place. I hated that I had to put her on my list of suspects who might be a part of the scheme to take me out, but I'd been betrayed by my wedding planner, and when your wedding planner turns on you, it makes it hard to trust anyone. "I'm having a real day of it, so keep your chaos to a minimum. Got it?" I asked, more tersely than I'd meant.

She frowned. "I really thought getting laid regularly would have taken that stick out of your ass." Then she smiled and put her hand on my arm. "I'm just messing with you. You look sexy as shit, by the way."

Cinnamon cream overwhelmed my senses as two

strong arms encircled me from behind. Immediately, I relaxed.

I patted Ford's hand. "Well, it's so nice seeing you, Carly. I appreciate you coming. We'll catch up later, okay?" After I figured out if she was one of the bad guys or not.

"You bet," my blonde cousin said brightly on a wink. "I wouldn't have missed this shindig for all the sweet tea in Georgia."

A brunette in a turquoise dress, ruched at the waist with a peplum hem, yoo-hoo-ed me from across the drawing-room. "I have to go," I said, grateful for the excuse to shorten my goodbye with Carly. "That's Sister Sandy, the high priestess performing the ceremony tonight. I better see what she wants."

The high priestess had been a holy pain in my ass, but I thanked the Goddess for the timely distraction as I departed from Carly and made my way across the room, my hand firmly clasped with Ford's as I dragged him along. I was not facing Sister Sandy alone.

I bumped into another guy I hadn't met before and prayed he wasn't another crazy relative. He had sandy-brown hair with golden highlights and dark gray eyes. He gave me an approving, flirtatious stare.

"Bride," I said.

"Guest," he said. "Ford's a lucky guy."

Ford took my hand. "I sure am. I didn't know you were back in town, Toby. Are your folks here?"

"Wait a minute?" I peered more closely at the man. "Toby Rosen?"

Toby smiled. "That would be me." Toby, a warlock I went to high school with, had been a wide receiver on the football team. In other words, we didn't run in the same circles. Like at all. But he had been friends with Ford.

When I didn't respond, he added, "Nice to see you again, Hazel. I'd heard you had moved back to town." He looked at Ford. "My parents couldn't make it, but when I heard the quarterback was getting married, I marked the date off on my calendar." He laughed and gave Ford a quick elbow nudge. "By the way, my folks told me to pass on their congratulations."

"Send them my thanks," Ford said. He gave Toby a clap on the back, and we moved past him.

"Talk about a blast from the past," I said. "What's he been up to since high school?"

"I have no idea," Ford said. "He and his parents moved to Florida about a year after high school."

"Huh. Well, as interesting as it is to catch up with old friends, we have bigger fish to fry." Sparks tickled off my fingertips.

"Ouch," Ford said, jerking his hand away. "Watch

the fireworks. And don't zap the priestess. She already looks like she's ready to bolt at any moment."

"Sorry, babe." I straightened my dress and tried not to sound as grumpy as I felt. "I'll behave."

Ford snorted. "That'll be the day."

My mood darkened even more when I saw Pierce Roberts—another warlock, and the town's CPA—a few feet from the distressed-looking priestess. "Good wedding to you, Chief Kinsey," he said. Pierce was not a fan of mine. He'd been friends with Adele Adams, a witch I took out when I first moved to Paradise Falls, and while he didn't say it, I'm sure he blamed me for the hellmouth in the middle of town last fall.

"Thanks, Pierce. It's nice of you to come tonight."

"I wouldn't miss a binding ceremony," he said. "It's a rush."

I wasn't sure what he meant by that since this would be my first, attending and having. "Okay. Well, I better get to Sister Sandy before she has a coronary. See you at dinner."

"Yes, you will." He gave me a tight-lipped smile then nodded to my mate. "Ford."

Ford gave him a curt nod back. "Pierce."

"Hey," I said when we finally reached the priestess. "Pretty dress. What's up?"

Sandy worried her purse strap between her fingers. "I can't find Vivi anywhere. Have you seen her?"

I didn't want to lie to Sandy. I'm sure it was against some rule somewhere to tell fibs to the Goddess' handmaidens. I cast a quick glance at the door under the stairs. "Nope. Haven't seen her." I was on the speedway to witch hell. "How come you're looking for her?"

"I'm embarrassed to tell you this, but my ceremonial shawl went missing this morning." Sandy's thin face pinched. "Vivi said she'd find it or arrange to get me a replacement. I really need it to properly sanctify your nuptials."

"Can you just…" I wiggled my fingers.

Sandy pressed the fingertips of her right hand above her left breast, the skin around the indentions blanched. She said in a reverent tone, "Heavens no, child. Each thread on the shawl is blessed by twelve priestesses. You can't just magically manufacture that kind of thing."

Meh. I didn't really care if the thread was blessed by twelve vestal virgins, Ford and I wouldn't be any less married, and that's all I really cared about. "I'm okay with you just doing a traditional human exchange of vows. If you can't find the shawl," *because Vivi cannot help you,* I added silently, "then we'll get married without it. No problem."

"Wrong," Sandy said. "Big problem."

Ford's grip on my hand tightened, and my fingers started to tingle. "What do you mean?"

"I'm sorry, Hazel and Ford, but if I don't have my shawl or a replacement in time for your binding, then I won't be able to perform your ceremony. It is a necessary part of the binding spell."

"Ow," I said, yanking my hand free from Ford's suddenly steely grasp.

My hostile mate narrowed his gaze at Sandy. "That is not acceptable."

"Again, I'm sorry," Sandy said, her aquiline nose raising an inch to meet Ford's glare with one of her own. "Let's just pray to the Goddess my hallowed stole shows up before then." She then passed me a look that I swear held a smidgeon of accusation.

"Yes." I crossed my arms, and the seam of my dress became excruciatingly taut against my backside. "Let's hope you find your shawl, and let's hope that I don't find my gun."

Sandy's eyes, dark violet in color, went wide. "What do you mean by that?"

Ford took my elbow more gently than he had my hand. "She's just edgy, your worship. We'll find your missing cloak before the end of the night."

Sandy huffed a breath but appeared somewhat mollified. "See that you do, or this binding is off."

Ford hustled us away before I could tell Sandy where she could stuff her worship.

"Hazel!" a woman shouted. It was Becksy's mother, Lena Ansel. Her short brown hair framed her wide cheekbones and large green eyes. She clasped my hand warmly. "I just wanted to thank you for allowing Becksy to participate in your ceremony tonight. She's thrilled to be one of the young witches launching the flower boat wishes out onto the lake."

The flower boat wishes were wax paper hats filled with flower petals. Casting them out onto the lake was a symbolic way of casting off single life moments before the attachment magic happened. I hadn't been single in a while, but I wasn't going to shortchange the town on tradition.

"I'm glad she agreed. She's a lovely girl. You must be very proud."

"I am," Lena gushed.

Mercy Langston moved in next to Lena. She gave me a sour smile. "Looking tightly wrapped tonight, Hazel. Be careful you don't have an accident."

"What?" That didn't sound suspicious at all. Sheesh.

Mercy quirked her head toward the stair. "You almost went splat over there. We wouldn't want carelessness to get in the way of tonight's festivities." She touched my hand. "You look nice."

When she sauntered off, Ford grabbed my hand again and dragged me into the dark, secluded coatroom.

"You were really pushing it with Sister Sandy out there. Are you trying to get turned into a toad before the ceremony?" The heat of his body warmed my skin and raised gooseflesh on my shoulders. He ran his fingertips down my bare arms. "Because I don't know about you, but I'm not keen on mating with an amphibian."

I leaned into him, pressing my boobs against his rock-hard abs. "She's not that scary. Mercy Langston, on the other hand..."

"You don't get to be a high priestess because you lack skills, babe. And as for Mercy Langston, well, she's made the suspect shortlist with her creepy warning." He caressed my cheek. "Goddess, you smell good enough to drink."

"My cup runneth over." I smiled at the borrowed quote, which had totally not been intended to be used as foreplay of any kind. "Why don't you come take a sip of all this goodness?"

Ford reached around my waist and lifted me up until my feet were dangling inches from the floor. He growled low and lustfully. "You know what a thirsty man I am." He kissed me hard, his lips melding hot against mine. I parted my lips for the welcome invasion of his delicious tongue and moaned. I tried to part my legs as well, but the stupid dress was so friggin' tight around my thighs, there was no wiggle room. Like at all.

Damn, my ovaries were turning blue as lusty yumminess made my lady bits throb with need. "Boy, howdy," I whispered when he eased from my lips. "Keep that up, and we won't make our own wedding dinner."

Ford chuckled at the end of a low, sexy growl. "Mom would never forgive me."

"And the mood is killed." One should never mention a parent mid-make-out session. "So, what do we think happened to Priestess Sandy's holy robe? Is that part of the conspiracy to take me out? Or a coincidence?"

Ford cupped my butt cheeks. "Damn, you got a great ass."

"And I'd like you to explore it more. Later. After we figure out who's trying to whack me."

"Maybe Vivi lied." Ford's lips brushed my neck. He sniffed my hair. "It is difficult to think with you this close."

A thrill zinged inside me. I loved that I had such a devastating effect on Ford, but now was not the time to get loved up. Even still, I had to fight the urge to climb him like a greased pole at the fair. The tight dress helped dampen my urges. I hated Vivi anew for making me buy this stupid thing because "the blue brings out your eyes—and the cut makes your butt look good." I sighed. "Maybe we should go somewhere less close-quarters."

He slid a hand down my thigh and then back up, his fingers trying to slip under the edge of the painted-on cocktail dress. He growled when it didn't slide. "I think we need to have a talk about wardrobe."

"You don't like the outfit?"

"I'd like it better on the floor."

"Goddess, Ford. I swear if you keep this up, I'm going to let you have your way with me, and then you can explain to everyone why the bride looks like she's been through a hurricane."

He grinned. "Deal."

I giggled and grabbed two handfuls of his face scruff. "You are incorrigible."

"I am a man in love, darling," he said roguishly. "Maybe we should have eloped."

"It's too late for that." Or was it? "Hmmm."

"I wanted to get you alone to talk, but damn, I can't think of anything but wanting to touch you. There are way too many clothes between us."

I rubbed my stomach against his hard groin. "I agree." His scent plundered me from the inside out, and at this moment, I couldn't worry about what it was he'd wanted to say.

"It's important," my bear moaned. "Goddess, Haze. You know how to turn me stupid."

"All that blood rushing from one head," I tapped his temple, "to the other." I squeezed his sausage.

"Exactly."

"Maybe you should tell me before you lose any more brain function."

"Too late for that." Ford inhaled me again, drawing a deep breath through his nose. Instead of the contented sigh that usually followed, this time, his nose wrinkled, and he frowned.

"What?" I lifted my arms and dipped my head to smell my pits. Nope. My vanilla bean and raspberry deodorant—I tried to choose fragrances that worked with the mating scent and not against it—was working overtime. "What is it?"

"There is a sudden faint stench in here." He set me on the ground. My buttocks mourned his touch. "I think it's coming from behind the coat-check counter."

I guess it was time to take off the bridal veil and put on my cop hat, but it really made me wish I had brought my cop gun. "Wait," I said. "What if it's a trap?"

"Why would an assassin lay a trap in the coat

closet? No one could have guessed we'd come in here."

Ford's logic was sound, even so... "Proceed with caution," I said. If it was a witch or a warlock, they could translocate away if we got the upper hand. But a shifter would be really dangerous in these close quarters.

"Every time," Ford replied.

We took two careful steps toward the smell. A quiet hiss had both Ford and me wide-eyed and alert. I held up my fingers and wiggled them. I mouthed the words, "Paralyze. Hold on." Freezing bad guys was one of the few spells I had semi-mastered.

Ford nodded.

"Freeze and stay.

No poofing away.

No hiding from me.

So mote it be."

A sizzle in the air was the extent of what we felt as a result of the spell.

Ford looked down at me and mouthed, "Did it work?"

I shrugged.

He gestured for me to go around the left side while he took the right. The coat check bad a five-foot counter with doors on both sides that led back to the storage area. We moved as silently as we could. Not easy with four-inch heels on hardwood floors. But really, I thought if someone was going to jump out at us, it would have already happened.

I opened the door on my side at the same time Ford opened up his.

We both let out a breath of relief when there was nothing but a large bundle of coats, jackets, and sweaters on the floor.

"Why are all these coats on the ground?" Ford asked. "And what is that scent?"

I saw a wood bar peeking through the end of the pile. "It looks like the rod fell down." I didn't have Ford's nose, so I wasn't sure what he was smelling. The look on his face told me it wasn't anything good. "Maybe a rat or something crawled under all those jackets and died," I offered hopefully. Goddess, you knew it was bad when you wished for small dead rodents and not large dead bodies on your wedding day.

Ford wrinkled his nose "This close, it smells like decaying flesh, but also a little game-y. Could be a rat," he agreed.

"Ew." I noticed a yellow square on the topcoat. A black satin trench with faux fur cuffs and collar. Who the hell would wear fur in July? "Is that a sticky note?"

Ford reached down and plucked it up. "It's blank."

I took the paper from him and turned it over with

my fingers. I felt a prickle of magic, very faint, so whatever it was, it wasn't a heavy-duty spell. "Stand back," I told Ford and set it down on the coat-check counter.

"You think it's a trap?"

"Probably not. Not enough mojo, but I can't be sure. So, keep a safe distance."

Ford took one little step back. "This is as far as I go."

I nodded. I loved that he was in for a penny, in for a pound, as the old-timers used to say. I took a step back as well, putting us hip to hip. I turned and looked up at him. He kissed me. "Let's do this."

I held my hand out and directed my will toward the yellow square.

"*Unseen seen. So mote it be,*" I incanted.

Lettering began to appear on the small square.

Hazel, no one else has to die. Only you. But if you need motivation, I've left a familiar gift for you under this pile of rags...

Familiar? Ford had said the smell was like that of a rat. My stomach went squishy, and I could feel my heart in my throat. My throat with thick and panic made me frantic as I yanked the coats from the floor, chucking them over my head...until I saw Vivi Lashay's body. The body that should have been rotting in the cupboard and was now in the coatroom.

I gasped at what I saw next.

Curled up beside Vivi was something red and furry. My pounding heart skipped a beat. I held back a sob as I dropped down to my knees since the goddessdamn dress didn't have any bending room and grabbed the red creature.

I let out a choking cry, cradling the dead squirrel in my arms.

"Is it Tisiphone?" Ford asked, his arm going over my shoulders. His use of her full name made me sob harder.

"No." I hiccupped and took a few deep breaths. "It's a squirrel-squirrel. Oh, Ford. It's so awful." I put the sad carcass on top of the satin coat and let Ford comfort me for a moment. "Whoever killed this poor creature is going to get a lightning bolt right up their ass."

His chest rumbled with anger. "And I'll rip off their arms for good measure."

"Thank you."

He smoothed my hair back away from my face. "What do you think this means?"

"I think it's pretty obvious. Someone knows Vivi is dead. And they are sending me a clear warning that if I don't die, they'll come after everyone I love."

CHAPTER 4

"GREAT GODDESS IN A GUN BRA, HAZE!" Tizzy, with dramatic flair, threw an almond across the Bride's Room in her version of a rage tantrum. She balled her tiny fists on her hips and glared at me. "We can't let them get away with this. We are dealing with monsters. What kind of jerkface would kill a poor defenseless squirrel?"

"A jerkface with a death wish." I didn't want Tizzy anywhere near this situation. I was sorely tempted to ask my dad to translocate her to Siberia until we caught the culprit, but I knew she'd never forgive me if I made that choice for her. "I promise you, Tiz, this asshole is going to get what's coming to him."

"Or her," Lily added.

"Or her," I amended. Vivi had been female, so it

stood to reason that the killer could be of any gender, and really, any species.

Lily's human beau, Parker Knowles, put his arm around her. "I've never been so confused," he said.

"It's all right." Lily patted his arm. She'd told me that he suffered from PTSD related to his military service. I could see his shoulders and his face relax at her touch. She leaned her head against his shoulder. "I told you things can get homicidal in Paradise Falls. It's just that kind of town."

"Now, Lily," I admonished. "It's not like we're the supernatural crime capital or something. Parker, if you want, Dad can take you back to Moonrise. There's no reason to put you in the middle of our hometown drama."

He shook his head, his light blue eyes, framed with dark lashes, alight with defiance. "I go wherever Lily is," he said. "If she stays, I stay."

"I can't leave," Lily told him. "Not until Hazel is safe."

"Then neither of us will leave. I may not have any magical powers or supernatural strength, but I am handy in a fight."

I admired Parker's willingness to put himself in danger for Lily, even if I thought it was misguided. Lily was better at taking care of herself more than anyone else I knew. Even better than me. I nodded. "Then you stay."

"This is the last straw," my dad said, his frustration reaching a boiling point. "Whoever this is managed to place a corpse in the cloakroom while you two were in there and leave a magicked note, all without notice. We need to stop messing around and call in a professional."

"I *am* a professional, Dad." Sheesh. "Ex-FBI. Current chief of police. I don't think it gets any more professional or qualified than me to investigate what's going on here." I gave him a pointed look. Speaking of the corpse... "Where did you stash Vivi, by the way?"

Dad grimaced. "Your house. I put her in the deep freeze."

"You put a body in the freezer?" Parker asked.

Lily met his gaze. "Regretting your decision to stay?"

"Nope," he said, but his stance was more rigid than it had been a minute earlier. Lily had told me her magical ability to detect lies didn't work on Parker, but sometimes body language was just as good as a polygraph. He was staying, but it didn't mean he was happy about it.

"What about all the meat in there?" Ford asked my dad.

Dad shrugged. "Thawing on your utility floor."

Tizzy skidded forward, a look of sheer panic on her cherubic squirrel face. "And my nuts? I keep bags of walnuts and pecans in that freezer."

"I might have left them in there."

"With the dead chick?" she asked, her eyes wide with horror.

My dad nodded. "Afraid so."

Tizzy shook her fist in the air and squealed, "Noooooo! Not the nuts."

I decided not to ask about the tubs of Chunky Monkey and Mint Chocolate Chip ice cream. Everything in that deep freezer with the body would be thrown into a pit and burned anyway. I couldn't risk dead-woman goo near my food. I did mourn the loss of the ice cream, though. First Vivi tried to kill me, and now, she'd ruined my ice cream. The woman had turned out to be a real sadistic monster.

Tizzy jumped up on the vanity. "I'll murder 'em!"

"Calm down, my love," a gray Persian cat purred. Her name was Lupitia, aka Loopy-poopy-butt and whatever other name I could think of that was unflattering, aka Tizzy's lady love, and she was currently my dad's new cat familiar. She'd been an unwelcome addition to my team, but Tiz had insisted her girlfriend be in the know. "Hazel already has trouble with simple multitasking. Your anger will just add to her confusion."

Did I mention that Lu-pain-in-my-ass is also my nemesis? We are BEFs, Best Enemies Forever. I only tolerated her because her love for Tizzy rivaled my own. If it hadn't been for that little fact, I would have turned her into a stuffed animal. I bared my teeth and held up my hands. "I'm happy to transport your furry rear end right out of here."

The cat, who was as fluffy as she was full-bodied, sat up straight. "Do not threaten me, witch." Her Slavic accent was thick when she got her back up. "You are terrible with magic. Your threats do not scare me."

I poked my finger in the cat's face. "Exactly. I am terrible. You might not go anywhere, but then again, you might end up on the moon."

Loopy-doopy, even with fur, managed to blanch. "Fine." She sighed as if bored. "I will keep my wisdom to myself." She rubbed her head against Tizzy's. "I just worry about my lover."

Gag. Hearing her call Tizzy lover was the equivalent of hearing that someone pooped on my bathroom floor. For the record, that only happened once, and it was a drunken beaver shifter who fully shifted and shat on the tile in the guest bathroom. Yeah. Good times.

"Don't be so hard on Lupitia," Tizzy said. "She's my girl. How would you like it if I ragged on Ford all the time?"

Ford's chest rumbled.

Tizzy waved her hand. "Fine. I'm the pot calling the kettle black. Let's move on."

Tanya Fudging Gellar, who had been blissfully silent up until then, said, "We need to get a list of everyone here."

"Good idea. Mom has a seating chart," Ford said.

I scowled. Yes, I was being petty. Tanya was with my dad now, no longer scheming to get my man, but still, there was something about Ford's approval that made the blonde witch sparkle. *Blech.*

"We need to eliminate as many people as we can from the suspect pool so that we can narrow our focus. There are thirty people here tonight. That's too many to vet in a couple of hours," I said. I looked at the clock on the wall. "It's five until seven. If we don't get downstairs and get seated in the dining hall, Ford's mom is going to send out a posse. And Lily, maybe you can poke around about Sister Sandy's missing shawl."

"You got it," she said. "I am on the case."

"Maybe we should stagger our departure. It might raise suspicion if we all go down as a group," my dad said.

"Who's going to be suspicious of a wedding party traveling in a pack?" Tizzy asked.

Dad frowned at her. "This is my first time trying to

cover up a dead body. Excuse me if I am rusty on the protocol."

"Dad, is there anyone you know who might be holding a grudge?" I hated to ask, but the sins of the parents and all. "I mean, did I invite my own assassin to the party?"

He pursed his lips. His unlined forehead wrinkled unnaturally as he contemplated the question. Finally, his face relaxed. "I can't be sure, pumpkin. Your mother and I had our share of run-ins before and after you were born, and she made some powerful enemies. But I don't know why they would have waited until now to take their revenge. It makes no sense."

"When we get the list from Ford's mom, make sure you mark anyone you think might need a second look."

He nodded.

"Okay, so I suppose we should all try to act as natural as possible during dinner. Interact with as many people as you can and make a note of anyone acting suspiciously."

"Wanting to harm you is not suspicious behavior," Lu-dead-to-me said.

Tanya snorted. I glared at her and the cat. "Either be helpful or go away."

Tizzy and Dad looked at their girlfriends and shook

their heads. Tanya managed to appear embarrassed. Loopidstupid maintained indifference.

I almost forgot about my ace in the hole. "Lily, can you use some of your powers of persuasion to get some truths out of people?" A significant spell gone wrong around Halloween had caused my werecougar friend to develop a latent witch talent passed down from her great-grandmother, who, it turned out, was a founding member of Paradise Falls. Lily could tell when someone was lying, and even better, the power encouraged people to be truthful with her when answering direct questions.

My BFF nodded, her green eyes bright with intensity. "These days, I'm better at detecting lies."

"Tizzy, I'd really like for you to skip tonight. Maybe go back to the house. Let my dad take you. Okay?"

"Not okay," she said. "I'm not leaving you with a lunatic on the loose."

"When I thought…" Grief caught in my throat. "I can't lose you."

She leaped from the vanity and flew to me. I caught her easily. Tizzy clung to my neck, her tiny nails scratching my skin. "I'm not going anywhere, Haze. You're not getting rid of me that easy."

I nodded. "I guess we all have a dinner to attend."

Ford's phone beeped. "Mom again," he said. "She wants to know where we're at."

"Tell her we're having sex."

"I guess everyone needs to skedaddle on out of here then." Ford winked. "I can't lie to my mom."

Lily laughed. My father cringed. "Please don't put that image in my head," he said. He made a circling gesture. "I think it's time we all go."

We staggered our exits and went two by two by four, with Lily and Parker joining Ford and me at seven on the dot. I'd like to think that I glided down on Ford's arm but being a cop in sensible shoes on a daily basis doesn't prepare you for an entire evening of stilettoes. I probably more closely resembled a lame camel on stilts. Thank the Goddess Ford was so yummy. All the people who would care, aka the women, whether I floated or clomped when we entered the ballroom for dinner had their peepers trained on my guy.

Eat your heart out, ladies. In his tailored suit, Ford looked like James Bond. Well, if James Bond had been a rugged mountain man. Most of the guests had taken their seats, with only a few people still looking for their names on the placeholders. I groaned when I saw my cousin Carly sitting on Patrick Edger's lap. Ford's best man was getting the royal treatment from the floozy in the family. Nita and Bryant Baylor, Ford's parents, were both red-faced, but Nita still achieved a smile when she saw us.

My aunt Morgan wore a pink jersey dress that hugged her curves. My second cousin Ezra sat near the cat shifter alpha, Mary Lowe. The two of them seemed to be having a lively discussion. Mike Crandall, the *paullulum mammalia,* aka tiny critters alpha, huddled in with some of the larger shifters.

I moved past Patrick to Ford's younger brother, Lincoln, who sat next to Becksy Ansel, a teenage witch he'd been dating for a couple of months. If body language was any indication though, I think the relationship was close to running its course. Awkward. You should never plus-one a new relationship months before an event. Also, disappointing. I'd really been rooting for the teen lovebirds.

The seat next to Carly and Patrick's hadn't been taken yet. Ugh. I did not want to sit through a four-course meal listening to her wild tales, or worse, watching her play grope-y grab-ass with Ford's best friend. Patrick, a weremongoose, was a really good guy and great to have around when you needed some surveillance work done. Those mongooses had a real knack for squeezing into tight spaces without being seen or heard.

Eventually, I settled on switching Gary Gary, first and last name, *a name so nice his parents named him twice* —at least that was the joke—and Rhoda Benson's names with mine and Ford's at the end of the table. It meant I'd be far down the table from Lily and Parker, which bummed me out. However, while sitting next to Carly would be painful, Gary Gary and Rhoda had been seated in the middle chairs on the long table. Which was perfect, because I'd be able to hear more conversations in a centrally located spot than way down at the end.

"Haze!" Carly exclaimed. She squirmed off Patrick's lap and into her seat. The mongoose excused himself from the table in a quick escape. Carly grinned at me. "You look anxious. You're not having second thoughts, are you? Oh ho! I think someone's feet are so cold they're frozen," she hooted. "Need a quick exit? I can levitate you right out of here."

"My feet are plenty warm." I squeezed Ford's thigh as he settled into the seat next to me.

Carly leaned forward and scoped out my bear. "I'm sure there are plenty of warm parts on you. Huh, sugar bear?"

Ford's eyes widened.

I changed the subject. "How are things in Kentucky?"

She really perked up then. "Raising hell, blowing shit up, and popping brains like zits. You know, the usual."

"Popping brains?" Alarm didn't begin to describe what I was feeling, but it was a good start.

"Not literally," she amended. "Well, only that one time…"

I cast a sideways glance at her. "I'm not sure I should hear this."

"Why?" She eyed me suspiciously. "You going to tell your gram on me?"

My gram, as Carly called her, was Grand Inquisitor Clementine Battles, aka the Battle-axe. Calling her "gram" was super bold and stupid on Carly's part. I mean, the woman put her own son in jail for almost two decades, imagine what she'd do to someone she didn't love. And since Grandmother was putting in an appearance for the ceremony, I didn't want trouble between her and Carly ruining my day—that was the next assassin's job.

"Maybe you can ixnay on the ramgay," I said discreetly.

"You have a gay ram here?" Carly asked, way less discreet. She twisted her neck back and forth, searching the guests. "Where? I've got to meet this dude."

"Goddess on toasted strudel, Carly. I was using pig Latin. There are no gay rams. I mean, there might be gay rams, somewhere, not here, because rams, goats and sheep in general, are not shifters, and I don't have any non-shifting furries at my wedding," I said, exasperated.

I heard a clearing of throats behind me, and about ten familiars, mostly cats, gave me the crappiest stares.

"Other than the familiars, of course," I amended.

Tiz leaped onto my shoulder. "There goes the familiar vote. Way to start your reelection campaign," she muttered.

I shushed her.

Carly's face split into a wide grin. It was frightening. "Tisiphone! As I live and breathe, girl. How are you doing?"

"Keeping it nuts." Tiz chittered. "I see you are, too."

Carly put her finger up in front of Tiz, and Tiz high-fived the digit. They both laughed. I forgot how well they'd gotten along. Crazy attracts crazy.

"Great." My smile felt tight. Constricting. "I have to check on the..." Great, I had no lie ready. "...uhm, find the priestess. I have to ask her, you know, questions."

"About the wedding night? Because if you need tips and tricks, I got a zillion of them." She pinched Ford's cheek. "I've been told I'm an expert."

"I can't hear this!" Tiz exclaimed. She jumped down from my shoulder and took off.

"I'm good." Ford and I took a step back, just out of her reach. I had hoped a more mature Carly would be less destructive, but my hopes were getting dashed by the minute. "Now, don't go blowing up the cake or anything," I told her.

Carly guffawed. "I hate to make promises I can't keep."

I laughed nervously, praying to the Goddess she was kidding. The table settings consisted of a salad fork, dinner fork, dessert fork, salad knife, butter knife, and a soup spoon. Linen napkins were folded like stars where the plates would go. There was a water glass, already filled, a larger goblet for tea or soda, a wine glass, and a champagne flute. Nita had planned a series of toasts to the bride and groom during dessert.

I scanned the room of witches, warlocks, shifters, and familiars, trying not to be obvious in my observations for anyone who might look like they were ready to pull out a knife or a gun or throw some lethal magic at me. Most everyone seemed to be chatting with their neighbors as they sipped water and nibbled on rolls from the breadbasket. Soon, the catering staff would bring out real drinks.

"Do you see anything?" I asked from the side of my mouth to Ford.

"Not yet." He slipped a piece of paper into my hand. "The seating chart. Mom gave it to me. She's not happy about you changing the seating arrangement."

"Well, I guess we could tell her we're about to feed

my potential killer. Or killers." I frowned. "You know it sucks that we might be providing sustenance to assassins."

My stomach gurgled, so I led Ford to our new seats and grabbed a whole-grain bun from the assortment, slathered it with butter, then added currant and blueberry jam. Little single-serve pots had been placed at each setting. The jam was my favorite. I took a bite and let the berry tart goodness coat my taste buds. "Mmm."

"Congratulations, you two," a man across the table said. He gave me an appraising look that told me he liked what he saw. It was the guy from earlier. The one who'd caught me before I'd splatted on the floor at the bottom of the stairs. Ford's hand tightened on my knee. My love was a possessive man, but since I felt the same way when a woman made eyes at him, I didn't hold it against him.

"Thanks," I said. "It's nice of you to come to the wedding." I saw the name David Declan on the placeholder in front of him. "Did you have to travel far, David?"

"I'm living in Rhode Island these days. I'm surprised you remember me. I think you were six or seven the last time I was in town." He smiled, and his straight teeth reminded me of Chicklets. Big, square, white, and shiny. I wondered if he magically enhanced them or if they were natural. "I haven't seen your family for a long time. It's good to get back home."

Until Ford, I'd never believed anything in Paradise Falls was worth coming back for, so it was surprising to find out that someone was happy to visit. "Do you have kin still here?"

"Yes, Cheryl Gellar is my sister."

Yuck. "Tanya's mom?"

"Yes." David smiled. "I heard Tanya was dating Kent. Interesting if it's true."

"Why interesting?"

"We knew your mother, of course. The idea of Kent dating my niece, well, it was surprising. Honestly, I can't believe my sister didn't try to interfere."

I shrugged. "Maybe she did." Damn. Had I been too wrapped up in my own stuff to see my dad going through his own melodrama?

"I don't think so. I suppose Cheryl thinks bygones should be bygones. Besides, fathers and daughters should know as little as possible about each other's love lives."

I laughed. "That's a true story." David was charming. He must have gotten the nice genes in his family. "Do you have a daughter?"

"No." He held up a bare hand. "It wasn't in the cards for me." David was cute and charismatic. If he hadn't been related to Tanya Gellar, I would have tried to set them up, mostly because I didn't want to call her Mommy.

When everyone was finally seated around the long table, the wait staff brought out little plates of garden salad and small bowls of cold watermelon soup. I barely got the first scoop of soup into my mouth when a scream, followed by silence, followed by alarmed voices, had me struggling out of the chair. Why had I picked such an unforgiving dress? Oh, right. I hadn't. Vivi no doubt picked it out so I couldn't run away while she was shooting me. "What's going on?" I asked when I gained my feet.

Lily found me first. "Oh, my Goddess, Haze. He's dead."

"Who?" I saw my dad and gave a small sigh of relief. "Who's dead?"

"Gary Gary." She clasped my hand. "He keeled over —right into his salad."

CHAPTER 5

"POOR GARY GARY. Maybe he choked on a cherry tomato," Lily said. "It just takes one wrong inhalation at the right moment."

"Nope," Tanya said, using her medical examiner voice. "Throat is clear." She stripped off her latex gloves.

Nita and Bryant Baylor had ushered all the guests back into the drawing room. Needless to say, no one was hungry anymore. And even if they were, who'd eat the salad now?

"Myocardial Infarction? Aneurism?" My BFF was stretching for some kind of natural cause.

"He's a warlock. He's not going to have either of those things." Witches and warlocks didn't tend to suffer from mundane human ailments. Which was super great, but it also meant that Gary Gary's death wasn't an accident.

"Lily, can you get some details from Rhoda?" I asked. Maybe she could shed some light on the events leading up to Gary Gary keeling over.

"Sure thing."

I loved Lily for not making this any harder for me.

Bryant Baylor, the stockier, shorter, grumpier, older version of my husband, stomped over to me.

"What is going on here, Hazel? And don't blow smoke up my ass. You and Ford have been secretive and scarce all afternoon. I know you're hiding something. Is Gary Gary's sudden demise part of it?"

"I," tried to think of good lie and failed, "really don't know. Honest. I don't know why he died."

"I think you're full of crap," Bryant grumbled.

"Dad," Ford warned.

"Oh, you know I like Hazel just fine, son. You and she make a good pair, but I know bull when I hear it."

"It's an official investigation," I said, finally coming up with a good fib. "I can't talk about it with a civilian."

Bryant scowled. "You're a bad liar, Hazel."

"I'm a great liar," I said defensively.

Ford raised a curious brow in my direction.

"But I don't make a habit of lying," I amended quickly. "Honesty is the best policy and all that."

"Uh-huh." My soon-to-be father-in-law looked less than convinced, but he let it go. "I better go help Nita calm the other guests. I was sent to tell you that an ambulance will be here soon to take Gary Gary."

"Thanks." Well, crap. There was no way to keep the second death on the down low, and frankly, Gary Gary deserved better than being stuffed in my freezer with Vivi. Unfortunately, my fairytale wedding was quickly turning into a horror story.

Lily returned a few minutes later. "Rhoda said Gary Gary had started sweating profusely, he complained about a headache and said his stomach burned. A few minutes after that, he complained about bugs crawling into the candles and then ranted about pink puffballs trying to suffocate him. That's when he went face-first into the salad."

"Do you think sudden insanity caused him to choke?" Maybe someone had placed a crazy spell on Gary Gary.

"I'm pretty sure he was poisoned," Lily said.

"How?" Common poisons like arsenic and cyanide wouldn't kill my kind.

Lily gave me a look of pure exasperation. "Didn't you pay attention in our witch studies class, like ever?"

I hated high school, and the witch studies classes were a pimple on the butt of my high school years.

"Rarely," I answered, giving Lily a look right back. "Just tell me what you think killed him."

She rolled her eyes. "Fine. My best guess? Nightshade. It's fast-acting in witches."

"In the salad?"

"No. It's a little bitter and tart, so it would've been hidden in something sweet…oh! The currant and blueberry jam. We should probably have it tested."

I gaped. "Not the jam!" That sealed it. The poison, if it was nightshade, had been meant for me. It's common knowledge how much I loved the stuff. I'd been known to lick containers clean.

"I switched seats with Gary Gary," I said, horrified. "He's dead because I traded places with him. How could I have been so stupid? I didn't even think about collateral damage."

Ford put his arm around me. "You couldn't know, babe. Besides, you didn't kill him. That blame lies with the murderer." He kissed the top of my head. "And while I'm outraged for Gary Gary, I'm grateful you're still breathing."

I agreed with him. I hated that Gary Gary was murdered in my place, but I still thanked the Goddess I'd survived another attempt on my life. "Is there any way to test for nightshade poisoning?" I asked Tanya.

"Nothing quick." She lifted Gary Gary's eyelid. "His pupils are wide and fixed." She plucked up his lip.

"Mucous membranes are dry. I think Lily might be right." She gave my BFF an appraising glance. "Smart girl."

Lils shrugged. "I paid attention when it came to all the ways possible to kill a witch." She flashed an innocent smile at Tanya, who blanched. At that moment, I couldn't have loved Lily more.

"I could try a reveal spell," I offered.

Tanya huffed. "Those are complicated."

I'd heard that from more than one witch, but as unpredictable as my magic was, I seemed to have a natural affinity for location spells, which amounted to the same thing as a reveal spell. "They are my only specialty," I told my soon-to-be horror-in-law.

I wiggled my fingers at the table.

"Poison, poison
Deadly bright.
Reveal nightshade
With hot pink light.
If death's herbs
Were meant for me,
Show it now,
So mote it be."

I had learned spellcasting during my years amongst humans from a *Witchcraft for Idiots* book, and apparently, *so mote it be* wasn't necessary to make magic work. I'd found that I'd gotten so used to it as part of the ritual that whenever I left those words off, my spells failed more than half the time.

Tanya gasped as the tablecloth where Gary Gary had been sitting began to glow hot pink, and so did the single-serving jam pot. Yes! I stuck my tongue out at her. Just a quick, neener-neener-neener. My spell had worked. And by the pink light coating Gary Gary's mouth and fingers, he had definitely eaten the poison. It was also on Tanya's hands and Lily's. Casual transfer from their examinations.

"That is motherflippin' gross," Carly exclaimed.

"Who let her back in here?" I asked anyone. "Carly, you need to go to the drawing room with the rest of the guests."

"Screw that noise," Carly said. "Your gram asked me to keep an eye on you, and when the head witch shouts jump, I ask how high." She put her hand to her mouth. "Oops. I wasn't supposed to tell you that part."

For a moment, I thought I'd heard her wrong. "Did you say Grandmother sent you to watch me?"

"Well, watch over you." She frowned. "Just a little. Sorta."

Anger bubbled in me. I automatically reached down to touch the gun I wasn't wearing. "What did she say to you exactly?"

"Carly, you should go to Hazel's wedding." Carly

sniffed. "I told her, hellz yeah! I mean, I live with four witches in a halfway house. This is like a four-star luxury. I plan to have a little hinky-kinky in every room, if you catch my meaning." She eyed Patrick meaningfully. He blanched.

Ugh. I not only caught it, I was afraid I was going to need a shot of penicillin to get over it. "Not the Bride's Room," I said, trying to keep the horror from my expression.

Carly nodded. "That'll be the first room I hit. I hear the bed is pretty bouncy." She giggled. "And since security is pretty loose at this joint..." She winked then looked over her shoulder, wiggled her butt and waved at Patrick. He looked away, but not before I noticed a spark of interest in his eyes. Goddess help us all.

Tizzy squeaked her disapproval. "This falls under TMI," said my little queen of TMI.

"So, my grandmother didn't say I was in danger or anything like that," I said.

Carly shook her head. "She implied it."

"How?"

"By telling me to come to your wedding." She blew a stray curl from her face. "I can read between the lines. I've even started to learn French."

"*Parlez-vous français?*" Tanya asked.

"Are you calling me out? Because I will explode a witch," Carly said.

Tanya shrank back. Reluctantly, I stepped in to help. "She asked if you speak French in French."

"Oh." Carly blushed. "I'm only at the boonjourney and wee wee."

"Got it." I widened my eyes to Tanya, and we exchanged a look that said, *that witch is cray-cray*. We didn't agree on much, Tanya and I, but on this, we were in perfect harmony.

Which made me think maybe my grandmother had just wanted to get Carly out of town for a minute. That, I would understand. But more than likely, the Grand Inquisitor knew about the bounty on my head. Then why send Carly? Why not send her investigators?

Nita Baylor sauntered over. She glanced down at the body and winced. "I've talked to the caterer. He said he can hold dinner for half an hour before the food is ruined. Do you think they'll have Gary Gary moved by then?"

"We have to cancel the dinner," I told her.

"No!" Nita's eyes widened with horror. "I spent almost a thousand dollars alone on the meal. We can't cancel."

Ford put his hand on his mom's shoulder. "We

think Gary Gary's death is a result of poisoning. We can't risk anyone else dying because of the food."

"But Jordan Masters comes so highly recommended. He's cooked for your grandmother, the Grand Inquisitor," she protested, but most of the fight had left her tone. "Fine. How about cocktails then?"

I shook my head. "I think we better keep to canned and bottled drinks for the time being."

Nita sighed, and I felt bad that all her careful planning had been destroyed. "Dying at a wedding dinner is just rude," she lamented.

"Nita," her husband admonished.

"I'm sure Gary Gary is sorry," Ford said.

Nita blanched, suitably chastised, and walked away, presumably to find canned soda.

High Priestess Sandy joined our group. "I've come to check on you both," she said to Ford and me. "I'm here if you need spiritual guidance." She held out her hands in a gesture of openness.

Ford and I gave each other a quick look then focused back on the priestess. "Oh, Sandy." I took her right hand in mine and pointed out the hot-pink glow on her palm. In my best Lucille Ball impression, I said, "I think you have some 'splaining to do."

CHAPTER 6

WE'D TURNED the Elysian Room into an interrogation space. It was smaller than the ballroom, more intimate, and there were no windows. Perfect for getting confessions. I'd had Ford call the station for backup to contain the guests and the staff working the event. There was some complaining by the caterer and his team, but I think most of our family, friends, and family friends were freaked out enough to comply without a lot of fuss.

Ford stayed out in the drawing room to coordinate the lockdown while Lily, my werecougar lie detector, sat next to me behind a small white desk. We put a chair on the other side for the interviewee. In this case, Sister Sandy.

"How did you get nightshade poison on your hand?" I asked her without any subtly. Witches, even high priestesses, could be excellent liars, and I hoped to catch her off guard with the blunt question.

The priestess' eyes darted nervously around the room. "I have no idea how it got there."

I looked at Lily.

"She's telling the truth."

"It could have been secondary contact. How many hands have you shaken today?"

Sandy's expression soured. "You mean other than yours?"

"I didn't poison the jam."

"Neither did I," the priestess said, her chin rising with indignance. "I only meant that I've shaken a lot of hands today."

"Did you wash your hands at any time?" I asked. The glow was too bright for it to only be a trace amount.

Sandy nodded. "Yes, of course. I...I had to tinkle after, you know. My bladder tends to be overactive during stressful times."

"Ah-hah." I slapped my hand down on the table. "And what has you so stressed out?"

She raised her brow. "Other than a paranoid bride with a penchant for drama?"

"Not cool, Sandy," I muttered.

"Neither is being treated like a murder suspect."

"Touché," Lily said.

"Et tu, Lils?"

She shrugged.

I turned my attention back to the priestess. "About what time did you last wash your hands?" A timeline for her hygiene would give me a better idea of when the transfer occurred, and hopefully it would narrow down the suspects, even if it was only by one.

Sandy puckered her lips and nodded. "It was right after we were all ushered out of the dining room. I used the restroom and washed my hands right after before returning to the guests."

So, the poisoner had contact with Sandy in the past hour. "Whose hands did you shake after that? Any of the workers or was it just guests?"

"Guests only. People were understandably upset and confused by Gary Gary's death, and I was doing my best to offer comfort to those in need. I had no reason to shake hands with the catering staff."

"Which guests?" Lily asked.

Her shoulders bunched defensively. "I don't know everyone's names."

"Calm down, Sister Sandy." The priestess wasn't from Paradise Falls, so her answer didn't surprise me. "A description of anyone you can remember will do."

Sandy looked at the wall for a moment, then turned her gaze back to me. She frowned. "You have to understand. I see dozens of people at these kinds of events every month. I'm ashamed to admit it, but I've stopped paying attention to faces." She waved her hand. Her bangles jangled with the gesture. "I recall a charcoal-gray suit, a pale green dress, and two blue dresses."

That wasn't helpful, considering I wore a blue dress along with half the women at the party. "Anything else? Height, hair color? Any distinguishing marks or tattoos?"

"Nothing that I can think of... One of them might have had brown hair. I'm very sorry that I can't be more help, but none of this is my fault. It feels like fate has it in for you." She pursed her lips and narrowed her eyes at me. "And I still haven't seen Vivi. Maybe you should go ahead and cancel the binding? My shawl is still missing, and as I've said before, I can't perform the ceremony without it."

"No. I'm not canceling the ceremony. I will find your missing shawl, okay?"

"You know, you're not any less married if you just have a regular wedding. Witches are not meant to tie their soul to another being."

Again, I was reminded of my mother's death. She and Dad had taken the binding route, and it had ended in disaster. But Ford and I were a different couple altogether. And Ford didn't have a choice as far as divorce went. The mating scent meant he would only ever love me. Binding my soul to his was my grand romantic gesture to say, *see, I'll only ever love you.* I never wanted him to doubt the longevity of my love. "I don't care if I have to tear this place apart, stone by stone, I will find your stupid blessed-by-a-thousand-virgins shawl, and I will be getting bound so tight to my boo that nothing can part us."

Sister Sandy cast me a flat look. "You're mixing your religions, but whatever." She waved again with a jangle-jangle of her bangles to emphasize her whatever. "I get paid whether the ceremony takes place or not, so I hope you do find it. Can I go now? I feel a migraine coming on."

"That's a lie," Lily said. She'd been relatively quiet until then. "You aren't having a migraine."

"Fine!" Sandy stood up. "You caught me. I don't have a migraine, but all these questions really are giving me a headache, and I want to leave. Now. Unless you plan to arrest me."

Lily shrugged and gave me a nonchalant glance. "I bet your grandmother could be persuaded to hold her for seventy-two hours. Maybe as a wedding present."

The priestess' eyes bugged.

I sighed. Heavily. While I couldn't arrest Sister Sandy for a white lie, it didn't stop me from wanting to throw the book at her for being a jerk. I was almost positive my grandmother wouldn't grant me any special favors, though. Clementine Battles was a by-the-book Grand Inquisitor.

I nodded to Sandy. "Don't do anything stupid, you know, like trying to leave." I was getting married tonight, even if I had to hold the priestess hostage.

After Sister Sandy exited the room, Ford opened the door. "Your father and I have been through the list, and we can't narrow it down. There's no one he can pinpoint as holding a grudge."

Lily shook her head. "Someone has it in for Hazel. And that someone is here. The note on Vivi's body and the dead squirrel are definitive proof that the culprit is here."

"Wow," I said to my BFF. "You're talking like a real pro." She'd moved to Moonrise to get away from death. It hadn't worked out like she'd planned, and Lily had been instrumental in the capture of several killers. "You should think about opening a private investigation business."

She chuckled. "I'm going to school to be a veterinarian technologist. The only mysteries I want to solve anymore is why Fido suddenly has explosive diarrhea."

"Ew." I took her hand. She'd had such a hard life since her parents' deaths. Losing her brother had been the catalyst that brought me back into her life. I'd hated seeing her leave Paradise Falls, but I would have given her up a thousand times to see her happy. "You really love your life now, don't you?"

"I really do." She cast her eyes toward the Elysian Room door. I knew her fella was just on the other side with Bryant and Nita. He hadn't wanted to leave Lily's side, but there was only so much witch-shifter business the coalition—including my soon-to-be father-in-law—would allow. "I love everything about my life."

"Parker's a good guy."

"He is, Haze. He's the best man I've ever met." Her eyes sparkled with emotion. "I'm so in love with him. I sometimes ache with how much I need him."

I squeezed her hand. "I know exactly how you feel. It's the reason why I have to make this ceremony happen. I don't want to wait another year to be officially bonded to Ford."

"I get it," she said. "And as your maid of honor, I swear to do everything in my power to make it happen." She gave me a reassuring smile. "Everything. Now let's find this poisoner and get you hitched. We have twenty-nine more guests and twelve workers to get through. Who's next?"

I tried to think of who might have a grudge, and while I could come up with about five witches off the top of my head, one stood out to me. Mostly because his dislike of me was no secret, yet, he came to the ceremony anyhow. "Pierce Roberts."

Lily scowled.

I nodded. "Yep. Let's make that A-hole squirm." And if it turned out he was guilty, I'd happily fry his 'nads off.

"This is utterly ridiculous, Chief Kinsey. I resent the implication that I poisoned Gary Gary." Pierce's face had gone an unflattering shade of red. "He's a doofus, but if I murdered people for being idiots, half the town would be dead."

Pierce Roberts was a certified public accountant, and he was privy to the financial situations of a lot of people in town. Not me, of course. I did my own taxes. Well, Tizzy did them, but I paid for the IRS software. "Gary Gary wasn't the intended target," I said. "I was."

"Why doesn't that surprise me?" Pierce asked.

"Maybe because you're the killer," Lily said.

The buttoned-up accountant glared at her. "Watch how you speak to your betters, Mason."

"I don't see any betters in this room," I said on a low growl that would make a bear shifter proud. I clenched my teeth. "Isn't that right, Lily?"

"Truth," she said, utterly unaffected by what Pierce had said to her. I wish I had her ability to hold her composure under trying circumstances. Unfortunately, she'd had a lot more years of practice dealing with these jackholes in Paradise Falls.

I clenched my fists hard enough that my nails cut into my palm. Lily shook her head, her eyes searching mine. "He's not worth it, Haze. None of them are."

I held my breath for a four-count then let it out slowly. "Did you try to poison me?"

Pierce shook his head. "No."

Lily nodded. "Truth."

"Did you hire an assassin to shoot me?"

Pierce's eyes widened. "Someone tried to shoot you? You really do attract danger."

"Just answer the question."

"No, I didn't hire someone to shoot you." He stood up and looked down his nose at me. "If I were going to take you out, it would be less...pedestrian."

I glanced at Lily.

She shook her head. "Truth. He's not our person."

"Can I go now?"

I shooed him away like a cockroach.

"This is going to take forever," I said. "The ceremony has to happen before midnight."

Lily pushed her cinnamon-colored hair back from her shoulders and said, "Then we better hurry."

"It might be more expedient to get everyone in the room at once."

"I'm up for it if you are."

"I love that about you."

By the time we got the thirty guests and the twelve employees lined up against the ballroom walls, many of the townsfolk coming out for the sendoff and ceremony had started to arrive. Ford instructed Alice Michaels, a deputy and shifter, to keep the new arrivals outside until we could examine everyone inside. And, as Sandy had reminded me, we still had to find the shawl. No shawl, no magical bonds.

I cast the nightshade spell again, and like pixie dust, our dinner guests all lit up in one place or another. The poisoner was no fool. He or she had made sure to expose everyone in some way to the deadly plant. Well, screw me sideways. I guess it had been too much to expect that our killer would wear a big sign that said, "You're Looking For Me."

It would have made a spectacular wedding present, though.

Tizzy and Ludiamondchiller raced over to me. "We found something," Tiz said. She leaped onto my back, her mini claws gripping the bandage dress as she crawled up to my shoulder. "It was in a fireplace grate."

"What did you find in the fireplace?"

My familiar jumped down and pulled a burnt multicolored swatch out of Ludicrous' collar. My heart sank. "Please don't tell me it's Sister Sandy's shawl."

My squirrel crossed her arms over her chest. "It's not Sister Sandy's shawl."

"Thank the Goddess."

She glared at me, her large almond-brown eyes giving me the "Are you some kind of stupid?" look.

"What?"

Tiz clucked her tongue against her teeth. "Of course, it's Sister Sandy's shawl, Haze. Don't be daft."

Great. It wasn't bad enough that assassins had infiltrated my wedding. Now, I had to contend with the destroyed magical shawl. "What am I going to do? Sandy can't join us without it. Apparently, it's been woven by the hands of a thousand virgin witches." Or something like that. My mind was blanking hard. I snatched the fabric out of Tiz's paw. "Maybe she only needs a little."

Tizzy stared at me.

"You never know! Gah! Why would someone do this?"

Lily bumped my arm with her shoulder. "Someone is trying to stop the ceremony."

"And succeeding," Tizzy added.

"What I don't get," Lily said, "is why a gun? Why poison? Why burn the shawl? A good spell could have taken you out long before now."

I looked at my BFF. Tanya had been right. She really was a smart girl.

"Why, indeed?" Someone was trying very hard to make the threat appear non-magical, but they had made one crucial mistake. The dead squirrel in the coat room. There was no way a shifter got past Ford without laying down a scent trail, so the only logical conclusion was magic. The killer's cruel trick had exposed them. I felt my lips turn up in a feral grin. "It's a witch or a warlock," I told Lily. "It has to be. Everything else is smoke and mirrors to throw us off." I waved and got Ford's attention from across the room, then announced, "You can let the furries go!"

CHAPTER 7

"NOOOOOOOOOOO!" Sister Sandy wailed. She held the minuscule remains of her magic cloth between her thumb and forefinger. "Whyyyyyy? Whyyyyyyyy? It'll take a decade for those stupid tailor witches to weave me another. This is how I make my living, for the love of the Goddess." She slammed her hand over her mouth. "Goddess forgive me."

I took a deep breath and tried to keep my voice even as I asked, "What do I have to do to get this ceremony back on track?" Inside, I was freaking out, evidenced by the uncontrollable sparks lighting up my fingertips.

"Calm down," my dad said.

"So not the right thing to say to a stressed-out witch who is as calm as she can be," Tizzy said, her high-pitched voice frantic. "You're going to get us all fried!"

"Where's Vivi?" Sandy cried. "Did she do this? Did she burn my shawl?"

"I'm pretty sure she didn't," I said. Though, really, there was no telling when the magical fabric got torched. "Where did you find it?"

Tizzy jumped up on my shoulder. "In the library hearth."

"I was in there this morning doing my blessing meditation." Sandy clutched her dress over her heart. "I made that room sacred. Who would defile it? Defile me in such a way? They will answer to the Goddess for this!"

"When?" I asked hopefully. Maybe the Goddess could just strike the culprit dead, and I could figure out how to get on with the night.

"Eventually," the priestess said. "You know. Karma."

"Oh, great, that unreliable bitch." I happened to know that what went around didn't always come around. If I was going to wait on karma to exact my revenge on whoever was destroying my wedding, I might be waiting a very long time.

My dad gripped my shoulder. "I think the time for subtlety is over, princess."

"You're right. Time to kick this into high gear."

I followed him back into the drawing room, where Carly was taunting the witch and warlock guests with threats of brain scrambles and exploding buttholes.

"Thanks," I said to my nutty cousin. "I'll take it from here." I gave my dad a *please help me* look. He nodded.

"Hey, Carly," he said to my cousin. "Why don't you wait outside until Haze is done here?"

She rolled her eyes but didn't give him a fight.

"Thank you, Dad," I mouthed as he gave me a final look before exiting.

Thirteen magical suspects scowled at me from the wall. Mercy Langston, Pierce Roberts, Selene Roberts, Lena Ansel, Cheryl Gellar, David Declan, Becksy Ansel, Mark Ansel, Toby Rosen, Petra Willoughby, Sister Sandy—who I made get back in line—Ralph Dean, Rhoda Benson, and Tom Parker. Most of them owned businesses in Paradise Falls, aside from the out-of-town guests and Becksy, who was a senior in high school. It was as if the entire Chamber of Commerce had come out for the dog and pony, or in this case, witch and bear show.

I'd grabbed Vivi's Walther PK380 from the Bride's Room earlier, and I pulled it from my Coach bag and tapped it against my palm. "So, which one of you poisoned the jam?"

"You've got to be kidding me," Mercy Langston said. "Are you threatening us?"

Cheryl Gellar snorted derisively. "Like mother, like daughter."

"What's that supposed to mean?" I asked.

The witch rolled her eyes but didn't answer.

Lily walked the line, ready to pounce on a liar, liar, pants on fire.

"First question. You can answer one at a time. Which one of you wants to see me dead?"

The thirteen suspects grew terribly quiet.

Tizzy said, "That question might be a little broad."

"Oh, right." Just because someone would like to see me dead, didn't mean they would actually go through with it. "Did you put poison in my jam?"

Every single witch and warlock said, "No."

I looked a Lily. She shook her head. I hoped her mojo wasn't on the fritz.

"So, none of you wanted to poison me?"

"What makes you think it was a witch or warlock and not a shifter?" Toby Rosen asked.

There was a rousing chorus of approval from the others.

I held up the gun, effectively silencing them.

"First, this gun. Second, the poison; and third, the burning of a sacred cloth." I smiled triumphantly.

Lena Ansel stuck her chin out. "I have no idea what that means."

Her daughter Becksy was quicker on the uptake. "Non-magic means of getting rid of a witch," she said. "Whoever is responsible wants to avoid witch jail if they get caught."

Exactly. Dark or death magic, or using legal magic lethally, would get you put in a magic-nulling cell, but using no magic to take someone out meant no magic police would be involved. Human jails would never hold a witch. Whoever was trying to kill me would basically walk scot-free if I didn't stop them. "Winner, winner, chicken dinner for the smartest witch in the room." Except for me, of course. Becksy smiled, though. "A shifter would have just tried to rip my heart out." I nodded my approval to the young witch. "You can go, Becks. I don't suspect you."

She smirked. "You don't think I could do it?"

"It's not that." I hid a pleased smile. This was a little girl I wanted on my team one day. "I just think there are a lot of years of rage behind whoever is responsible. Your mom might qualify, but you haven't lived long enough to be homicidally angry."

Her mother, Lena Ansel, let out an angry huff.

"See what I mean," I told the teenager. "Years of rage."

Becksy pursed her lips. "Oh, I don't know. I've

thought about killing Lincoln once or twice in the past week."

"We can talk about that later." I looked at the time. Ten forty-five. Crap on a crackhead Goddess. The one-hour ceremony had to start at eleven for the magic to work at midnight. I wanted to cry again. It didn't matter anymore. Not really. Even if I managed to solve my murderous mystery in time, Sister Sandy couldn't create our bond. What was the point?

Carly came in when Becksy left. Mr. Ansel breathed a sigh of relief, and it made me feel terrible for the waving the gun around in her presence, but I was a desperate bride.

"I don't know who did the poison thing, Haze," Carly said as she scoped out the suspects. "But I get empathic vibes sometimes, especially when the emotion is strong. Someone is full of hate and violence. It's hard to say exactly who, but I'm going to guess it's one of the dudes though. The energy just feels masculine."

Carly was full of exciting surprises. It made me wonder if my grandmother really had wanted my cousin here to help me when trouble struck. Which meant, of course, that my grandmother had expected me to have trouble at my wedding. Thanks for the heads-up, Gram.

I nodded, trusting my gut that Carly was probably

right. "Okay, the ladies can leave. The room, that is. Don't leave the property."

"This is too much, Hazel Kinsey," Lena said. "If anyone runs against you for chief, I plan to fully fund their campaign."

"Is that so? Do you want to make it to the top of the suspect list?"

Mercy Langston did not wait to be asked twice. She walked out of the ballroom like her feet were on fire. Lena, on a scoff, and the other ladies followed close behind, except for Sister Sandy.

The high priestess launched herself at the men. "You will drink acid in hell, you shawl-destroying assholes!"

"Sister Sandy!" I gasped. "Carly, can you get her out of here?"

"I'll take care of her," Carly said.

My eyes widened. "Don't do anything crazy."

"No worries, Cuz. I'm not planning on doing anything fatal. Killing a priestess is bad juju."

"Awesome." After she ushered the insult-spewing priestess out of the room, I turned on the five remaining warlocks. "Do we keep playing games, or do I go psycho-bride on your asses?"

"Psycho-bride has been achieved," Pierce Roberts said. "So, by all means, let's quit playing games."

I tapped the pistol against my thigh and locked gazes with Pierce until he looked away.

"I don't have to put up with this, Kinsey," he said. "You are overstepping your authority."

He was going to wish I was only overstepping when I buried my stiletto in his backside.

"I agree with Roberts," David Declan said. "We didn't come here tonight for anything other than to witness a witch binding. If you really believed this was witch or warlock related, you would call in the Grand Inquisitor."

Humph. Fine. I changed my tactics. "Look, I'm just a girl, standing in front of a bunch of suspects, asking them to come clean about why you're so determined to ruin my special day." Ten-fifty. Dang it. Time was ticking away. "So, come on. I don't know any of you well enough to warrant this kind of crap. Why do you want to hurt me?"

"I don't," Pierce said. "I don't like you, but that's not a crime, is it?"

Unfortunately, it wasn't.

"I don't want to hurt you, Hazel," Toby volunteered. His eyes shifted to Lily.

She nodded. "He's...not lying." Even so, my BFF looked like she wasn't sure she believed what she was saying.

"Is it a half-truth?"

"No," she said. "He's telling the truth."

David nodded. "Same. I don't have a problem with you. At least I didn't."

Mark shook his head. "I kind of want to hurt you right now, but I'm not behind all this."

Ralph shrugged. "I've got no beef with you, Chief."

Finally, Tom said, "Ditto all that. I'm not behind this. Besides, I really liked Gary Gary."

I looked a Lily. Her face pinched with anxiety. "All truths."

Damn it! This was getting me absolutely nowhere.

Carly came running back into the room. "Get your wedding dress on, Haze! I got Sister Sandy a new shawl!"

CHAPTER 8

"WE'VE ONLY GOT a few minutes to get this shin-dig started," Carly said as she, Lily, Tizzy, and, surprisingly, Tanya rushed me up to the Bride's Room to hurriedly dress me for the female procession. Tanya used magic to enhance my makeup and my hair. The men would be doing the male version of the pre-ceremony ceremony in Ford's Groom's Room.

"You have a great crowd for the binding," Tanya said. "I still can't believe my uncle came. He's not a fan of your family."

"I think you're probably the only one. Your mother thinks I'm the devil."

"No," Tanya said. "She just thinks you're not qualified to police a town full of witches who are better at magic than you."

I glared at her. "Well, don't hold back, Tanya. Tell me how you really feel."

"We don't have time for a pissing contest," Tizzy interjected. "Not if you want to get hitched."

"I don't like this," I said. "We still don't know who's after me, and we have about three hundred people outside who I am putting in danger."

"Whoever is doing this wants you dead before your binding. This might be our best opportunity to flush them out," Lily said.

"Your skinny friend is right," Carly agreed. "Besides, I'm pretty sure the old Battle-axe has planted some of her super-troopers among the guests."

Great, that didn't sound dangerous at all for the innocent bystanders. "Is she here?"

No one answered, which meant she wasn't. If Clementine Battles had arrived, the whole place would be buzzing.

"Are you ready?" Tizzy tapped her tiny wrist. "Time's a tickin'."

"I..." I fluttered my lashes to keep them dry as tears threatened to spill over. "This isn't how I thought my wedding would go."

Tiz climbed up on my lap, she reached up and caressed my cheeks with her tiny little fingers. She had a cream-colored bow on top of her head that matched my gown. "You are not going to be any less bonded no matter how many people we have to kill to get you there."

I sniffled. "I didn't kill Gary Gary." I pouted. "Besides, you hate Ford," I blurted. "How is this going to work?"

"I love you, you foolish witch. And Ford loves you, which makes me not hate him. And you love Ford, which makes me actually love him. I am in this with you, Haze. I may not have said this before, but it doesn't mean I don't mean it. I am happy for you."

"Aww, Tiz." I dabbed at my eyes.

"You're smudging your makeup," Tanya said. She dabbed the corner of her own eye. "You have a strange relationship with your familiar."

"Tisiphone, I'm happy for you too. Even if I never say it again." I'd never live it down with Luwithaview. "You're my family." I looked at Lily. "Both of you. You've been my rocks. I don't think I could've gotten through this day without you."

"The day's not over," Tanya reminded us. "It's eleven o'clock. Let's get going."

One hour to wedded bliss. "I wish the other shoe would drop already."

"Maybe the interrogation scared the person behind the assassination attempts into stopping. Maybe there is no other shoe," Lily said hopefully.

"I'm digging the optimism, Lils." I looked up at my friend. "But do you really believe that?"

Her smile faded. "No, but a cougar can hope." She sat down on the bed next to me. "I love you, Hazel. I'm sorry your day hasn't been sunshine, rainbows, and unicorns. It should have been."

"The women are coming to usher you," Tanya said. "Get up and be ready to take your blessings."

I nodded. It was time to put my big girl panties on. I forced my fears down where they wouldn't distract me and stood up.

Tanya opened the door. Nita, Becksy, Joy Decker, Aunt Morgan and nearly a hundred more women, some I knew by name, some I didn't, some shifters, some witches, and all dressed in their best clothes, had lined the hall, the stairs, and the path to the lake. Lily preceded me with Tizzy in her arms.

Nita, who was first in line, had agreed to act in my mother's stead. She gave me a reassuring smile and held out her hands. I took them. We pressed foreheads.

"Blessed binding," she said.

"By the grace of the Goddess," I responded, then moved on to Becksy. Nita, as the mother of the bride, took her place behind me.

"Blessed binding," Becks said when we touched foreheads.

"By the grace of the Goddess," I said again.

Twenty minutes later, my neck had a kink from touching foreheads with shifters and witches. Toward the end of the line, I saw Carla Wells, the raccoon shifter who'd been in love with Danny Mason, Lily's brother. She looked different, happier than the last time we'd met. Lily stopped, and I could see her fighting to keep her composure. She and Carla exchanged nods as we moved on down the line.

When we reached the end, Nita retook my hands. "May your life be filled with joy and promise. This is my unending hope." She leaned in once more, touched her forehead with mine, then kissed my cheek. "I'm so proud to have you join my family."

"Thank you, Nita. I'm proud to be your daughter."

"It's time to go now," Lily said. She smiled, her green eyes full of love for me. She gestured toward the beautifully lit gazebo at the end of a path surrounded by hundreds of townsfolk, where my dashing Ford waited for me. It was perfect, just like his love for me.

I took Tiz from Lily and carried her on my left arm and linked my right arm with Lily's. "Let's do this."

My dad waited outside the door. All the guests along the path, men and women, touched me, murmuring blessings as I passed. I wanted to enjoy the beauty and magic of my community coming together to strengthen the ceremony, but I couldn't help but fear one of the many hands reaching out to me could be holding a weapon.

The clear night sky sparkled with stars as the full moon seemed to shine down on me like a spotlight. I slowed when we were only thirty or so feet from our destination. Ford stood under a coronation of white roses woven into the open-roofed gazebo. Damn, that man took my breath away.

Sister Sandy stood facing me on the other side of Ford. Lincoln and Patrick Edger stood with Ford as his groomsmen. Tanya took a seat in the first row of chairs. Tiz and Lily both kissed my cheek, and Lily took Tizzy to the stage. My dad turned to me. He looked scared.

"You okay, kitten?"

I choked on a laugh that threatened to turn into a sob. "I should ask you that question. You look like you swallowed a bug."

He nodded and pressed his forehead to mine as he took my hands the way Nita had. "You'll make this work, Haze. You won't be a disaster like your mom and me."

I nodded.

"You're better than both of us. You always have been, and Ford will love you. Always."

"He better," I said as a tear spilled down my cheek. I'd been so angry with my dad for so long that I hadn't even realized that I'd forgiven him. When had that happened?

"Thanks, Dad. I love you." I gave him a rare hug. "I'm ready."

"I know you are."

We began our father-daughter walk toward my mate. The ritual would last for at least fifteen minutes. Lots of incantations and such, but the final bonding moment had to happen at midnight exactly.

"This is really happening," I whispered to my sugar bear when my dad handed me off. I'd wanted this for so long, and considering the way the day had started, I had been confident it wouldn't happen.

He stroked his fingers down my arms, raising goose bumps along my skin. "You're so beautiful, Haze. I'm the luckiest man."

"You're not so bad either, hot stuff." We'd really pulled it off. We hadn't found the assassin, but the wedding was on. Thank the Goddess Carly had found a shawl.

Sandy cleared her throat. "Good people of the town of Paradise Falls, we are gathered here tonight to witness the union of two souls. Hazel Marie Kinsey and Ford Harvest Baylor have both agreed to enter this pact willingly and with joy. What magic and love bind together, let no one break asunder." The high priestess took the magic shawl and wrapped it around Ford's forearm then took the other end and tied it around mine.

She pivoted toward the lake. Dozens of teenagers launched their flower boat wishes onto the water. *"Woven souls, mind to mind, willing partners, souls to bind,"* Sandy incanted. My arm began to tingle, and the sensation tickled. I giggled. Ford's smile made me want to raise my flag on his pole. He was so getting molested the minute this binding was concluded.

"Heart to heart, always entwined, love forever, souls will bind," the priestess continued. She repeated both phrases over and over. I could hear dozens of guests join in the chant as power surged through my body, creating a pulse of magic weaving itself between Ford and me. The euphoria overwhelmed me, and I had to fight to stay on my feet.

I picked up the incantation, Ford began to speak it as well. I could hear Lily and Tizzy now, too. Everyone was smiling, laughing, as the ecstasy of magic poured through the field. Now I knew what Pierce Roberts had meant when he said a binding ceremony was a rush. This magic felt like the best drug ever.

"Souls will bind," I said for the hundredth time, feeling loopy and loved up. It was almost time. Midnight would be here soon, and Ford and I would never be parted.

Then the other shoe dropped.

CHAPTER 9

A CRACK of thunder followed by a hot breath of wind ripped between Ford and me. I dropped to the deck, the shawl falling between us. "Ford!" I shouted as panic clawed at my chest.

The thunderous noise had been a rifle shot; the heated air, a bullet.

"I'm here," he said, grabbing my arm. "We're sitting ducks on this platform. We have to move."

I heard splashing, and a few unGoddess-like words spew from a wet Sister Sandy's mouth. Thank heavens she'd survived. Ford and I rolled together as another shot tore through the wooden base where we'd just been.

"Swim to the bank, Sandy! Don't try to get out on the deck," I yelled.

She shouted a few more curse words, but I heard

her swimming—well, more like splashing—away from us.

Most of the crowd ran for cover, not that I blamed them. There was such a thing as collateral damage. After all, Gary Gary had suffered an innocent's fate.

Ford and I took cover behind a dense bush. "Do you see the shooter?" I asked him.

"No," he said. "But we need to get moving. This plant isn't going to stop a high-speed rifle round."

I shook my head. "We need to get this jerk."

Parker dive-rolled in behind us. "Where's Lily?" he asked, his eyes scanning the nearby area. "I haven't been able to track her since after the first shot."

Oh no. If anything happened to Lily or Tizzy, I'd never forgive myself. Never. "We'll find her," I reassured him. I stood up to get a better look around.

Ford tried to yank me back down. "In that dress, you're a bright target on a dark field," he shouted.

"I have to find Lily and Tizzy. I won't let anyone else go down for me. I'm not playing his game anymore." Another crack split the night. I twisted as the bullet grazed my arm. "I. Have. Had. Enough!" I bellowed.

Another shot had me changing my mind. I flattened myself to the ground next to Ford. "I am so frying this dude." I raised my hand and focused all my energy on the sparks sparkling from my fingertips.

I reached out and began a spell.

"Goddess give me what I need

To stop this assassin with hasty speed.

Give me strength to end this spree.

I ask this of you, so mote it be."

Flames shot down my arms as powerful energy full of rage and vengeance washed over me. Another shot whipped over our heads. Parker began to low-crawl toward the dock.

"Cover me!" he shouted.

"Go, go," I told him. "I've got you." I jumped to my feet and threw up my hands as the next shot was fired. The bullet stopped two inches from my palms then dropped to the ground.

I walked forward. Copper rounds bounced away from me in a quick one, two, three succession. Until the fourth one made it through and whizzed past my shoulder. Up until that point, I'd felt invincible.

"Hazel, the magic can't stop the mundane. Not for long. Get behind something, now!" my dad bellowed.

There had been a pause in the shooting. If I had to guess, the guy was probably reloading his weapon. I looked behind me for Ford. He wasn't there. "Ford!"

My dad grabbed my arm and dragged me away, out of the open. "Ford took off up the hill. He went after the shooter while you distracted him. Now you do your part again and stay safe."

I saw Parker. He was still searching for Lily. Goddess help me. My heart sank in my chest. "I have to find Lily and Tizzy."

Toby Rosen ran over to us. "I saw your friend. She's just beyond the stone wall just on the other side of the rose garden. She and your familiar ran over there to get out of harm's way."

"Where?" I asked. "Show me."

Toby nodded and directed the way, and I scrabbled behind him. My dress caught on a chair anchor and ripped. "Goddessdammit!" I hissed as I settled in next to Toby behind the barrier.

The firing had stopped. I heard someone shout, "He got him! Ford got the shooter. It's the freaking caterer."

I should have known. He'd been Vivi's recommendation. But so had the florist and the bartender, and as far as I knew, they hadn't been homicidal.

Still, relief flooded my bones upon hearing the celebratory cheers. I hadn't realized how afraid I'd been. Not for me, but for my friends, my family, and the life I'd started here in Paradise Falls. Finally, I'd felt home at home, and home was something I never wanted to lose.

I looked around but didn't see Tizzy or Lily. "Where are they?" I asked him. "Are you sure they were here?" Had they moved to another location? Maybe they managed to take cover in the house.

Toby shrugged, then shook his head. "I'm sorry, Hazel. I didn't—" Toby's eyes widened as I felt a cold blade against my neck and heard the menace in the voice behind me.

"I had a fiancée once," the man said.

I recognized the voice straightaway. Tanya's uncle, David Declan. "Why are you doing this, David?"

Toby looked frightened.

I gave a slight shake of my head. "Toby, you should go. This doesn't have anything to do with you."

"I had a fiancée," he said again. "But thanks to your father, she died on our wedding day. Make one twitchy move, Chief Kinsey, and I will slit your throat."

The cold blade bit into my throat as Declan emphasized his threat.

"Why do you think my father's responsible?" I asked. My dad wasn't a killer, unless you included my mother as a victim, which I did not.

"Shut up," he hissed. He gripped me tighter. So much for stalling tactics. I could try to apparate away, but I might put myself into a tree or at the bottom of the pond. Besides, David could slit my throat before I could get out two words of the spell.

Nervous sparks danced on my fingertips, and

Declan pressed the blade in hard enough to break the skin.

"Don't," he said. "I will kill you before you have enough flame to light a match."

He obviously wasn't the shooter if Ford had taken the guy down. Another hired assassin, probably. David Declan hadn't wanted to do the deed himself, but desperate times... "Why are you doing this, Mr. Declan? You don't seem like a cold-blooded killer." If he had been, I'd already be dead.

"I'm not a killer," he said. "Not like your parents." His hands were shaking now, but he didn't ease up on the blade.

I was both disturbed and relieved. Declan didn't want to get his hands dirty. He sought to hurt my father, but not enough to do it himself.

My nerves caused another ripple of sparks over my skin.

"Ow," he said. "I told you to stop that."

"I'm not doing it on purpose." I really wasn't. Sheesh. "How did my parents kill your girlfriend?"

I wasn't sure I wanted to know, but I had to keep Declan engaged.

"My soul mate," he corrected me. "The love of my life." He turned me to face toward the gazebo. I hoped Toby took the opportunity to run.

He pointed the knife toward the lake, and it was a

relief to have it off my neck. "We were standing right over there on that same gazebo as you were, ready to take our vows, when a lightning storm out of nowhere began to throw bolts all over the lake." His voice trembled. "Tilda was struck with a direct hit straight through the heart."

Had his fiancée been the bride Lily had mentioned earlier? If she was, I still didn't understand why he blamed my dad. "How is that my dad's fault?"

"Cheryl called me after you killed Adele. She told me the truth about the wild storms in Paradise Falls, and it wasn't hard to put two and two together. The monstrous druidic magic they were performing caused that lightning storm. They killed my baby girl."

"My dad was never a part of that," I said defensively. But my mother had been one of the founding members. She and her partners, using druidic magic, had been responsible for a lot of deaths. "When he found out about my mom, he put a stop to her."

"Kent's always been good at worming his way out of consequences. He should have rotted in Salem. I might have let you live if he had."

"Haze?" I heard Ford shout. He was looking for me.

I tried to call out to him, but Declan covered my mouth, put the blade back on my neck, and dug the tip in deeper. I felt a warm trickle of blood run down my skin. "Don't," the grieving warlock said. "Just don't."

My father started yelling next. Soon there were several voices, including Tizzy's, Lily's, and Tanya's. A tension eased inside me. My family and friends were safe.

I bit the palm of his hand and, and when he yanked it away, I seethed, "You won't get away with this. You might not end up in Salem, but Ford will never let you live."

"I'm okay with that," he said.

I saw Toby out of the corner of my eye. He looked like he might do something stupid, like an ill-timed rescue attempt. I gave him a slight shake of my head and mouthed the words, "Get help."

Toby nodded. I had a brief moment of relief...until I noticed he wasn't moving away.

"Go," I mouthed.

Toby smiled and shook his head. He put his finger to his lips. Was he going to get all heroic on me? Goddess, he was going to get us both killed.

"Why aren't you back in the crowd, Tobias?" asked David. "You can't claim innocence if they catch you here."

"I need to know that Kent suffers for his part in Tilda's death," Toby said quietly.

"My dad didn't have anything to do with any of the stuff my mom was doing. He tried to stop her."

"Not hard enough," he said through gritted teeth as he met my gaze. "You see, Tilda was my big sister. I admired her so much. She was always there for me, and because of your parents, I lost her. Declan called me after he found out what your parents did. That they were the reason she's gone." He reached inside his jacket and pulled out a gun. Crap. It was the Walther PK380 Vivi had tried to use on me.

How in the world had he gotten the gun?

As if reading my mind, Toby said, "I've always been good with translocation magic."

It had never occurred to me to try to protect the gun from getting spelled. Most witches didn't use mundane weapons, but these warlocks were determined to kill me with non-magic means.

Crap. I was well and truly screwed.

CHAPTER 10

"LOOK, you two. You haven't actually killed anyone yet. You can still get out of this with your life. You haven't used magic to do any harm. You can come back from this." I couldn't believe I'd bought into Toby's act. He'd lured me to the stone wall, so that he and David could get me alone. Smart move for a dumb guy. "You should let me go. You both can just poof out of here."

Toby lowered the tip of the gun, but David Declan tightened his grip.

"I'm okay with not coming back from this," he said. "Tobias, you should go. Tilda wouldn't want this for you."

It was a little late for that, I thought, but if it got rid of Toby, I'd go with it. "He's right, Toby. You don't want to ruin your life this way. You should go. Grief can drive us to do terrible things if we let it."

He shook his head. "I want to see this through."

Great. Toby was committed to revenge.

I raised my voice, hoping one of the people calling my name would hear me. "You ruined my binding. Isn't that enough vengeance for one day?"

"Hazel!" my dad shouted, his voice closer now. "Hazel!" I saw him then, along with Ford, Lily, Parker, the Baylors...they were all looking for me, but it was as if I were invisible.

"Why can't they see us?" I asked.

David chuckled. "I cast a cloaking spell."

Crap. He had crossed the line. He'd used magic for ill, which meant he knew, even if he didn't kill me, his magical goose was cooked. I had to figure out a way to be seen.

"Ouch. Cut it out with the finger zaps," David said.

"I can't help it," I told him. "It happens when I'm stressed out or afraid. Right now, I'm both those things."

He was hesitating. Stalling. Why? Either he was waiting on the right moment, the one with the most dramatic effect, or he hadn't yet found the courage to push the knife deeper into my neck. I needed a distraction.

A roar of warrior rage thundered over the lake. It was my man, and he was Big Bad Bear angry. Declan and Toby both looked away, their gazes tracking toward the sound.

It was now or never.

I let go of Declan's forearm, squeezing tighter against my chest. I dropped my hand down to my side.

"Fire and flame,

come to me.

Burning hot,

so mote it be."

Flames burst from my hand in a spectacular display, blue and hot, until it smelled like roasted warlock and singed hair.

Declan screamed as his pants caught fire. He tried to jab me with the blade, but I ducked out of his hold. Toby was startled enough to lower the gun and rush in to help. I blocked him with my arm, then kicked him in the gut. The fire from my right hand sprayed out from me as if I held a flame thrower. Toby staggered back from us.

"Ford!" I hollered. "I'm here!"

I was holding both men at flame's length.

"Unseen seen,

so mote it be," I said.

My bear—in bear form, I might add—saw me and ran toward us at a gallop.

"You guys are in trouble now," I told them.

"How?" Declan asked. "How did you break my spell?"

"I have a talent," I told him.

Before Ford could get a claw on someone, I piercing, "Aiyeeeeeeeeeee!" sounded as my flying squirrel swooped in and landed on Declan's head. She poked her claws into every orifice his face had.

A werecougar and a human crashed into Toby. Lily's massive paws pounded him, while Parker held him down for the beating.

Tizzy jumped into my arms as my bear rammed David Declan and took him down as well.

An explosion brought all fighting to a halt, and I heard Carly, say, "Get your ass back on over here, Sister Sandy, and do your job before the next explosion happens between your ears."

Nita Baylor hollered, "Five minutes. We still have five minutes! Get to chanting, Sandy, before I pummel your holy butt."

Ford, the bear, looked ready to bite a warlock's head off, but my dad stopped him. "Don't kill him," he said. "He's suffered enough."

Declan had given up the fight, his whole body shaking with sobs.

Toby hadn't quite come to terms with losing, though. "No!" He knocked Parker away, and even with

Lily clamping her powerful teeth down on his shoulder, he managed to aim the gun at my dad.

A fireball the size of a watermelon exploded right in front of him, throwing Toby back about twenty feet. We all stared in horror for about two seconds. I scrambled to my feet. I expected to see Carly where the fireball had originated, but no—it was Tanya Fireball Gellar. Her normally well-styled hair was in strings around her face, and she was sweating enough for a football team at homecoming.

She let out a squawking sob and ran to my dad. She threw her arms around his neck and kissed him over and over. "No one messes with my guy," she finally said. "No one."

Respect. Tanya had taken my dad's side over her own uncle. Huh. The witch really loved him. And hey, the thought didn't make me nearly as sick as it had before.

"One minute!" Nita shouted. "Ford and Hazel, get over here now."

My bear shifter, who was now back in human form, and completely naked, picked me up in his arms and ran to the dock, where a very befuddled and stressed high priestess incanted the chant in high speed. My dad threw the magic shawl over me and tied it back behind Ford's neck.

This was happening. Oh my Goddess. My skin

tingled and my heart threatened to burst from my chest at any second. The remaining twelve or so people, including Parker Knowles, chanted like their lives depended on it. Tanya had her hands on my neck where Declan had cut me, healing me. Wow, maybe I'd died, and this was what witch heaven felt like. I must have been judged worthy because I was getting everything I ever wanted. When did crap like that happen?

Ford kept brushing my hair back, kissing my face, my neck. His arms tightened around me. "So scared," I heard him mutter. "I can't. I can't… Never lose you, baby."

Goddess, he must have been out of his mind with worry. "I'm here," I told him. "Safe in your arms. Where I'm meant to be. Always."

"Ten seconds!"

Sandy sped her chant up even more, sweat dripping down her forehead. Or maybe it was water. After all, she had jumped in the lake. This was a woman with a strong sense of self-preservation.

"Four, three, two, one!" the crowd roared.

And that's when it happened. I swear light from the moon shattered something inside my body, and for a brief moment, I felt the swarm of Ford's love cradling my entire being. I felt elated. I felt whole. I ran my fingers through his thick, chocolate-brown hair, drank in his gorgeous blue eyes, and said, "Now, you can't get rid of me, hot stuff."

"You've thwarted my plan, vixen." He smiled. "I love you, Hazel Kinsey."

"Hazel Kinsey-Baylor," I corrected him. He kissed me then, long, languid, and sensual. Full of love and lust and a promise of hot, sweaty monkey sex. I felt his pool noodle rise to the occasion.

"Goddess in a furry thong, I'm going blind," Tizzy exclaimed. "Put your bear necessity away, for the love of nuts."

I heard Parker and Lily laugh with joy. Ford and I joined in. We made it. We beat the odds. For once, Paradise didn't fail.

The next day...

"Are you sure you don't want to come to Moonrise while Haze goes on her honeymoon?" Lily asked Tizzy.

My familiar shook her head emphatically. "I'm not going to spend two weeks running away from your four-legged drool beast."

Lily giggled. "Smooshie is just playing with you."

"Like a cat plays with a mouse," Tiz quipped. "Forget it. I'll be fine here. I'm going to stay with Kent."

"Oooo," Lily teased. "While the witch is away, the cat and squirrel will play."

"The cat and squirrel play even when the witch is here," Tiz said.

"That's more information than I want to know," I told them both. I hadn't had enough sleep or enough coffee to handle the morning's conversation. Ford had taken Parker to the lake this morning, so I could spend time with Lily before we parted again. Ford really did love me, and the fact that Parker didn't take much persuading even though it was painfully clear he hated to leave Lily's side, told me he loved her as well. "You and Parker make a cute couple," I said.

"Uh-huh." She eyeballed me suspiciously over her latte.

"He was pretty good in a fight."

"You're not wrong," she agreed.

"So, are you guys planning to," I touched my wedding band, "seal the deal?"

"What do you think will happen with David Declan and Tobias Rosen?" Lily asked in a not-so-smooth subject change.

"I guess they'll be tried and put into witch jail. They did use magic, which technically puts them in my grandmother's reach."

"Speaking of your grandmother, I thought she was coming to the wedding," Lily said.

"Yeah, me too." I sighed. I'd been disappointed when she hadn't shown. I didn't have a lot of close family members, and while we didn't have a standard grandmother-granddaughter relationship, I had still hoped she would show up. "She's a busy woman."

As if I'd conjured her, Clementine Battles appeared in my kitchen, her silver hair swept back into a severe bun, her white pantsuit sharply pressed and impeccably tailored.

She smiled when she saw Lily. "So nice to see you again, my dear." She turned to me next. "Hazel," she said, a note of fondness in her tone. "I'm so happy your ceremony was a success." She shook her head. "Sad about Gary Gary, though. Still, I thought you handled yourself very well last night."

"I did, huh?" Like she would know. Carly probably called her right away with a detailed report. "I'm sorry you weren't there to see for yourself."

Clementine smirked. "But I was, dearest Granddaughter. I was there the whole time."

"I think I would have known if you were at my wedding. Someone would have freaking noticed."

My grandmother's gaze narrowed at me. I could feel myself withering under her stare, then suddenly, she said, in a voice I recognized all too well, "Well, spank me blue and call me Nancy if it isn't my favorite cuz!" The look on my face must have been genuinely comical because my grandmother, the Grand Inquisitor, actually laughed. "I wouldn't have missed your wedding for any reason, Hazel. But I wanted the day to be about you, not me. And, as Carly, I could help protect you. Clementine Battles has to be neutral and unbiased, but Carly can be as biased as she wants to be." Her eyes softened at the corners.

I threw my arms around her and said something I never thought would come out of my mouth. "Thank you, Grandma."

"You're quite welcome," she said and returned the hug.

The End

Get FurOut (Witchin' Impossible Book 5) today!

Familiar allies. Old friends. New enemies. And a dead werewolf. Paradise Falls has never been hairier.

Paradise Falls, I'm the law and crime here is about as common as a good hair day in a tornado, and peace between shifters and witches has never been smoother. My familiar, Tizzy the squirrel, keeps me entertained with his acorn-fueled antics, while my bear shifter hubby, Ford, makes me feel like the safest witch on the planet.

I should've known bliss never lasts. Like a vegan at a barbecue, trouble rolls into town in the form of a pack of werewolves. These furry interlopers aren't here for the scenic hikes or the artisanal honey—oh no, they want a piece of Paradise Falls, and they're not asking politely. When the Witch-Shifter Coalition votes to boot the wolves, the head howler throws down the gauntlet, declaring the sacred *Rite of Arphlitian*—a ritual fight to the death as ancient as the town's oldest oak tree.

With no choice, the town must choose a champion. And guess who volunteers? Yep, my honey-bear, Ford. As the new mayor, Ford steps up to the challenge, determined to defend our home.

But when the alpha werewolf is found dead, all paws point to me as the prime suspect. I'm sure someone in town is conspiring with the newcomers to take down the leadership in Paradise Falls. But who? And to what end?

Unfortunately, in Paradise Falls, the only thing more magical than the town's charms is this mystery.

Find out what happens NEXT for Lily Mason and Parker Knowles in Pit and Miss Murder, book 4 in the Barkside of the Moon Cozy Mysteries!

FUROUT - SNEAK PEEK

Chapter One

The morning sun streamed through the window as I settled into my worn leather chair in my cluttered office. A harsh ray of light crossed my desk, drawing attention to the doom piles of paperwork I'd been avoiding all week. My coffee, a strong brew with a punch of cinnamon, sat steaming beside a half-eaten donut.

Being Chief meant paperwork, people management, and politics. I'd scheduled a little one-on-one with the new mayor to discuss the police budget. The new guy was handsome and sexy, and it would be the highlight of my day. I looked at the time. Ten in the morning. Ugh. My meeting wasn't until two. Four long, tedious hours away.

The dispatch radio in my office was on for background noise. This morning there had been reports of a fender bender on Main Street, a noise complaint from Mrs. O'Malley's familiar again, and Officer Daniels managing traffic near the high school. Mundane, everyday police work in a town that had, in the past, been fraught with horrific murders, shifter-witch conflicts, a gaping tar pit to hell in the middle of Main Street, and enemies from the past rearing their ugly, revengeful heads. It was shaping up to be a typical morning in Paradise Falls.

In other words, I was bored out of my gourd.

I sighed heavily. "What I wouldn't give for a minor dustup. Nothing too catastrophic, but enough to get me out of this office for a few hours."

There is an old adage that goes, "Be careful what you wish for." It's an adage for a reason.

Our newest rookie officer, Becksy "Bex" Ansel, ran into my office. "Chief Kinsey, you need to hear this." The other officers started calling her Bex, rationalizing that Becksy was too cutesy of a name for a tough cop. I had full confidence in the young witch. Her skills as a police officer were as impressive as her magic.

"What's up?" I responded, eager for something mildly interesting to break up the morning.

Her perky nose twitched. "There's trouble out at the Junkyard Dog."

Junkyard Dog, an ironic name since the last owner Clayton Driver had been a cat shifter, was down a rough gravel road on the Merry County line. The location also made it a perfect spot for criminal activity. Half the property was on Lister, the county that bordered ours, which made it a nightmare for law enforcement, considering jurisdiction was always in question. Still, it had been closed and unoccupied for eight years. Ever since Driver met his maker after trying to kill my best friend, the property had been about as lively as a sloth on vacation.

Less eagerly, I asked, "What kind of trouble?"

"Detective Edger called in on a private channel. He says there is a large group of unknown and dangerous-looking shifters with what looks like moving trucks heading to the Junkyard Dog," Bex answered, looking flustered.

I frowned. Patrick Edger, a weremongoose I had appointed the head of special investigations, had his nose and ears to the ground in Paradise Falls. If he said the group was unknown and dangerous, I believed him.

I got up and moved to the front of my desk. "Not good." Newcomers to Paradise Falls were rare, and anyone showing up without an invitation was immediately suspicious.

"He wants to know how you want him to handle the situation," Bex said.

My first impulse was to send a patrol car to investigate the strangers, but shifters could be unpredictable when challenged, even when you knew them well. I wouldn't send any of my officers into the potentially volatile situation until I had more information.

"Let's hold off on doing anything for a minute. Ask Patrick to observe from a distance. No direct contact with the strangers," I instructed. "I need to make a call."

She nodded and hurried back to her desk. I picked up my cell phone and dialed the mayor's number. He answered on the second ring.

"Hey, hot stuff." The newly appointed mayor, who also happened to be my dear husband, Ford Baylor, said in a low and seductive voice. "What're you wearing?"

I grinned at my mate's welcome audacity. "A nine-millimeter."

"Mmm," he growled. "And nothing else?"

I choked on a laugh. "As much as I want to finish this conversation," I replied. "And I do plan to finish it later, we've got a situation at Junkyard Dog, and since my best officer up and quit on me..."

"I didn't just quit, Haze," he said gently,

"I know," I told him. "I just miss having you

around all the time." Being mated was more than just a signature on a piece of paper. It meant I always wanted to be wherever he was, holding on and loving him for the rest of our lives. Since Ford was a shifter, the feelings were even more intense for him.

"I miss you too." His tone was tender and reassuring. "Tell me about this situation. What's been reported?"

I sighed. Back to the business of business. "There is a report of new shifters in town. A whole group of them, apparently." I kept my voice steady despite the anxiety gnawing at me.

"New shifters?" Ford's surprise was palpable. "This is the first I'm hearing of it. They should've petitioned the coalition for an invitation before entering town. What are they up to?"

"That's what I'd like to know," I told him. "Patrick Edger says they have moving trucks. It makes me think they plan to stick around. Whatever their intent, they are trespassing on property that has been abandoned for a long time, making me even more nervous. Who owns the Junkyard Dog now?"

"I'll call down to records and find out whose name is on the deed." Ford was silent momentarily, and I could almost hear the gears turning in his mind. "Haze, we need to approach this carefully. I don't want a confrontation without knowing more about them."

"I agree. But we need to find out who they are and why they're here." My witchy senses were tingling. "I have a bad feeling about this."

"I do, too," he said. "But let's not rush into anything. I'll call a meeting with the Witch-Shifter Coalition. Maybe someone knows something about these new arrivals. In the meantime, I want you to hold off on approaching them directly. Let's see if we can gather some information first."

"All right," I agreed reluctantly. "But we can't just sit back and do nothing."

"I know," Ford said. "We need to play this smart."

"Understood," I said, feeling itchy. "If they are playing by shifter rules, they'll be expecting someone to show up and ask questions."

"If they were playing by shifter rules, they wouldn't have shown up unannounced," he countered.

"True." Still, I couldn't let the incursion into our town go unanswered. "I'll be the picture of diplomacy."

"Uh-huh," Ford said, unconvinced. "Don't go alone. Take a few of your witch officers as backup. Leave the shifters far enough away that interlopers don't see it as a challenge."

I nodded even though he couldn't see me. "Good tip."

I could hear the rasp of his breath for a few seconds before he added, "Just promise you'll be careful."

"You got it," I assured him. "Let me know as soon as you find anything out, and I'll keep you updated on my end."

"Check in often," Ford said, his voice softening.

I looked out the window at our sleepy town and across the street at the courthouse. Ford was looking out his window at me.

A small smile tugged at my lips despite the tension. "I will."

He placed his large palm on the window. "I love you."

Like a two-barrel shotgun, my heart double-pumped. Our mate bond was locked and loaded. "I love you, too." After the call ended, I slipped my phone back into my pocket. When I turned around, I let out a little yip, sparks of magic shooting from my fingertips.

Sitting atop one of the paperwork piles, a large red, flying squirrel cracked an acorn as she stared at me.

"Don't sneak up on me."

"I've been here for like two minutes," she said, her voice high and feminine. "I can't help it if you got the observational skills of a blind mole."

"I haven't been on the phone for two minutes."

"You've been moon-eyed staring across the road at

Fozzy the Bear since I popped in," she begged to differ. "You know your time blind where that man is involved."

She wasn't wrong. It was one of the many reasons he decided to run for mayor. Since our wedding, neither of us was worth a damn at our jobs when the other was around. "Don't you have a restaurant to run? Won't Lupita be short-handed without you?"

Lupita, a pearl-gray Persian familiar that Tizzy had fallen in love with, had inherited her ex-witch Romy Quinn's restaurant after Romy went to jail for dabbling in dark magic and nearly destroying the whole town. Lupita was now my dad's familiar, but she and Tizzy had their own tiny house together on my property. Ford and I had a few acres surrounding our Victorian home, and setting up a tiny house so we could all have some needed privacy was a small sacrifice.

"Lupita has it handled."

"I have a lot going on today, Tiz. Tell me what you need and make it quick."

"I need you to tell me what you're going to do about the pack of wolves setting up territory in our area."

I narrowed my gaze at her. "Werewolves? What makes you think they are wolves?"

"I dated a lone bitch once," she said. "You don't

forget the distinct scent of lycanthropy easily." Her whiskers fluttered as she sniffed. "They are selfish jerks. Trust me when I say you don't want their kind here."

"When did you date a wolf shifter?" I asked. "That seems like something I would've remembered. And how in the world? Logistically, it seems like a sizing nightmare."

"I've been around longer than you, Haze," she chittered. "I had a life before you. Several of them." She gave me a withering stare. "And I haven't always had this form, not that it's any of your business."

I put up my hands. "Fair enough." I often forgot that my familiar had a long, long history. It was easy to assume that she came into existence at the same time as I had, but that's not how it worked for her kind.

I gave her a go-ahead nod. "Okay, Ms. Werewolf Expert, if you had to guess why they are here, what would it be?"

She shrugged her tiny shoulders. "Secret shifterology cult? New age yoga retreat? Alien invasion?"

I chuckled. "Let's hope it's not aliens, Tiz. I don't want to have to explain to the coalition why crop circles are showing up in town."

"Whatever the reason, it's for sure going to be terrible," she quipped.

It made me wonder just how badly her werewolf girlfriend had jilted her. It was a story for another time. Right now, I had a pack to check out.

"Bex!" I hollered, and the young witch, work boots thudding on the linoleum floor, came running into my office.

"What's the plan, Chief?"

"I need every available witch officer to meet us at the Junkyard Dog."

"Us?" Bex asked. "As in you and me?"

"Yes, us," I told her. "I could use a strong witch in the field, and it will be good experience."

Bex hadn't been assigned a patrol partner yet, but I thought the girl had the makings of a good detective. Her years as a waitress at Lolo's Diner had given Bex a keen insight into shifters and witches and what motivated their behavior, whether it was food or crime.

Her back straightened, and I could see she was pleased. "Got it, Chief. I'll radio all available units."

"Witches only," I reiterated. "We're going to see werewolves, and I don't want anyone accidentally starting a war."

She clicked her heels together, her arms rigid at her sides as she pivoted and hurried back down the hall.

"Goddess in a pair of orange Uggs," Tizzy hissed. "For a minute, I thought she was going to salute."

"Leave the poor girl alone. She's excited."

"She won't be for long," Tiz said.

I had never met a werewolf in my life, and I didn't love the picture Tiz was painting. "It's really that bad?"

"Yep. That bad." She nodded emphatically. "As Jeff Goldblum once said in one of the Jurassic Parks, and I'm paraphrasing, but when it comes to werewolves at first it's all oooing and awwwing, until later when it's all running and screaming."

As I took my weapon from the gun safe in my office, I prayed to the goddess that the running and screaming was a joke and not a premonition.

Get FurOut today!

PIT AND MISS MURDER –
SNEAK PEEK
BARKSIDE OF THE MOON COZY MYSTERIES
BOOK 4

When Lily Mason's uncle is accused of murdering a prominent Moonrise citizen, the amateur detective and

her loyal pit bull Smooshie must dig out the truth and find the real killer.

Integrating isn't easy for a shifter in an all-human town, but Lily Mason is finally making it work. She has love in her life, enjoys a great job, attends community college, and best of all, her fixer-upper house is nearly livable. She couldn't be happier.

Until her Uncle Buzz is accused of murder.

A prominent member of the community has been found murdered in the parking lot of her uncle's cafe, The Cat's Meow. And thanks to a contentious relationship with the victim, Uncle Buzz is the number one suspect.

Now Lily, Smooshie, and the Moonrise gang must solve the murder before Lily's only family ends up behind bars.

Chapter One

"What do you think, Lily? Veil or no veil?" Theresa Simmons sat at the office desk in front of the computer and pointed at a sleeveless wedding gown on a bridal website.

I filed April's expense sheets and closed the cabinet. Thanks to a large donation of four-thousand dollars the month before, along with our regular donors, the rescue had managed to have a little extra left over to put finishing touches on the new shelter Parker Knowles, the owner of the Moonrise Pit Bull Rescue, had started building two years ago. Between fundraisers, volunteer efforts, and some directed donations, Parker's vision to save as many of these beautiful animals from awful circumstances looked to be a reality.

We finally had our new permits in order, and next week, we planned to move our current nine rescues over to the new place after Parker and a whole team of helpers finished the fencing for the outdoor play spaces this weekend. I was most excited that we'd have room to take in another fifteen furbabies until we could find fosters or forever homes for them. I hoped our open house, not this coming Saturday but the next, would raise a lot of money and get more people interested in volunteering or fostering.

Watching the transformations of the rescues was like living a lifetime in a few months as they went from injured, damaged, starved, and sometimes very ill dogs into energetic, loving, trusting, and healthy babies ready for forever homes. Not all of them turned around so fast, but even furkids who had trouble finding a way to trust, like our shelter mascot Star, who had been with us for over a year and a half now, deserved to be treated with love and kindness, whether they were ultimately adoptable or not. Parker and our team of pit bull lovers were virtual magicians, and their devotion to rescue gave me hope every day.

Last night, he'd taken in a year-old pup whose inflamed skin hung loose with severe mange that had taken most of his hair. So other than a black nose, we weren't sure of his coloring. The poor boy had trembled, his tail tucked and his head down. Parker stayed with him until early this morning. I'd been with Parker for Sunday Night Spaghetti, a weekly thing for us, when the call came in. I helped him with the paperwork and getting the isolation room ready. After, I'd stayed the night at Parker's house (for the fourth night in a row), and when I got up, I went over to take the morning shift so he could get some sleep.

Parker had been cuddling the sick dog and whispering words of encouragement. The pup's tail wagged when Parker had told him what a good boy he was, which had been a big improvement from the night before.

If I hadn't been in love with Parker already, that scene would have sent me all the way into my feelings. As it was, my heart had felt full to bursting. We'd been an official couple for almost a year, and our dating anniversary was fast approaching. He knew who and what I was, a cougar-shifter with a traumatic past, and it hadn't scared him off. Well, not after he'd had a minute to process, and by a minute, I mean the longest four months of my life. But here we were, going on a year, and I'd never been so happy. Frankly, it scared the heck out of me.

The dogs in the shelter, as if reminding me of how happy they were to be here, too, suddenly began barking with excitement.

I peered at the clock. It was noon. Lunchtime. Which meant Keith Porter, one of those awesome volunteers and Theresa's boyfriend, had probably just taken kibble back to them.

"Lily? Did you hear me?" Theresa asked, snapping her fingers to get my attention. "Veil or no veil?"

I rolled my eyes. "I think you should get a divorce before you start planning your next wedding."

"Spoilsport," she said. Her lower lip jutted into a pout. "Why won't you let me dream?"

"I'm happy to let you dream." I grabbed my purse. "I'm off to dream myself."

"That's right. You start summer classes today." Her expression soured. "I'm not sure how I feel about you getting all educated," she teased. "Next thing you know, you'll be too good for the likes of us."

"I'm too good for you now," I replied. This was my

fourth semester doing general studies at Two Hills Community College. If all went well this summer, I could start the Veterinarian Technician program in the fall.

"Well," Theresa said on a laugh, "then we're really in trouble!"

I giggled. "I'm not going anywhere anytime soon." As long as Parker wanted me around, there was zero chance I'd leave. Besides, I hoped my education could be a resource for the shelter. After all, I would be qualified, as long as I worked under the supervision of a vet, to provide care for the dogs we took in. I gazed at Theresa. "You know, it's going to take at least another year before I get my associates degree, and another two if I want to be a technologist."

"If?"

"Technicians can do just about everything a technologist can, and I can start practicing sooner." I shook my head. "Either way, I don't plan on giving up my duties here at the shelter." Although, juggling full-time classes, my shifts at the shelter, and Petry's Pet Clinic had been a time-management nightmare. I worried sometimes that my relationship with Parker would suffer, but he had been nothing but encouraging and supportive.

Theresa stood up and embraced me. "I'm glad." Her

voice choked with emotion. "I don't know what we did before you got here."

"Are you okay?"

Theresa wiped at her eyes. "I'm fine. Just happy."

I narrowed my gaze at her. Emotional, talking about marriage, demonstrative, and she'd been using the bathroom more frequently. "Are you pregnant?"

"How in the world do you always do that?"

"So, you are?"

"Yes." She hugged me again. "Keith is so excited, but we have to keep it under wraps until the divorce is final. Three more weeks! I can't wait to get that bastard out of my life for good."

"I'm happy for you," I told her, and I was. But I was also worried. Jock Simmons was a Grade-A jerk and a wife beater, but he was also a smart-as-a-whip lawyer. He was still on the town council, even after he'd been turned into a pariah when he'd smacked Lacy Evans at the hospital a little over a year ago, and he'd been arrested for assault. That took an incredible amount of pull. It was the first time Theresa's dad, Sheriff Avery, had seen Jock as an abuser. When the sheriff had confronted Theresa about it, she'd told her dad everything. It had given her the courage she needed to finally leave Jock.

Unfortunately, Jock had managed to get the charges knocked down to a misdemeanor and had only had to pay a fine. Rotten bastard. Jock's standing as a council member and as a family lawyer to over half of Moonrise, along with Lacy's reputation, had made it hard to get a felony conviction. And, since Jock was a top-notch in his field, he knew all the tricks to make Theresa's divorcing him next to impossible.

I worried this pregnancy would give him the ammunition he needed to make sure she ended up with nothing but the clothes on her back.

Still, I'd rather be naked than married to Jock Simmons, so Theresa would still be better off than before she'd left him.

"You and Keith will make amazing parents," I told Theresa, because regardless of the battle to come, I believed they could weather it.

She smiled. "Thanks, Lily." Her smiled turned into a frown. "You won't say anything, will you?"

"Cross my heart," I said.

Jordan Deeter, a college student majoring in graphic art and one of our newest volunteers, knocked outside of the office door. Her blonde hair was pulled back into a ponytail. She wore jeans, a pink T-shirt that said Show Me Your Pitties, and a pair of hot pink, chunky-soled, lace-up tennis shoes that gave her a slight height advantage over me.

In other words, she was a shorty like myself, only where I was built like a stick, Jordan had curves for days. I envied her as much as I liked her. Recently, though, I think she'd started using vinegar as a hair rinse, or maybe for feminine hygiene. Either way, I'd never been keen on the scent, so it rankled my nose. Still, I wasn't going to be rude about it.

"Hey, girls," she said. She held out a handful of mail. "This was in the mailbox. I hope you don't mind that I brought them in."

I took the small stack of mail from her and shuffled through it. Electric, phone, junk, junk, and an envelope marked *City of Moonrise, Department of Permits, Licensing and Inspections*, and it had the words, *Important: Needs Immediate Response*, stamped across the front.

"Thanks," I told her.

"Is everything okay?" Theresa asked.

"Sure," I said. At least I hoped so. The inspection for the new facility was a week away, so I couldn't understand why we were getting notified, or what it could be about. I opened the letter, the paper hissing as I pulled it apart.

Inside was a notice from the City of Moonrise that the rescue, the current shelter, was being cited for zoning violations regarding overgrowth of flora near the fence, spalling, and chipped paint. And it gave an appeal date but warned that we could be fined up to two hundred dollars a day in fines from date of issue until these issues were fixed. On top of that, if we appealed, there was a chance the fines could go up to a thousand dollars or more.

I groaned when I saw the date of issue. It was five days ago. It was signed by E. Laverty, Zoning Compliance Officer.

I swear if I'd been a teapot, steam would have whistled from my ears. "Son of a garbage eater."

Jordan joined us at the desk. "What's wrong?"

I slammed the letter down. "We're being cited for nuisance violations."

"Why?" Jordan asked.

"I have no idea. We passed our licensing inspection two months ago, but according to this, we have weeds along our fence and chipping paint." I pointed to one word I wasn't sure of. "And spalling? What in the actual heck is spalling?"

"Broken concrete," Theresa said. "Usually a sidewalk." She appeared a little gray as the color left her cheeks. "Oh, gosh, Lily. I think this is my fault."

I stared at her. "How in the world is this your fault?"

"Clem Hanley is the chair of the zoning commission. He and Jock are old law school buddies. This could be retaliation."

"But why would he come after the rescue?" Jordan asked. She might have been new here, but Theresa's separation was town talk. When both Theresa and I turned our gazes on her, she blinked sheepishly. "I'll go see if Keith needs any help."

After she left, I turned my attention back to Theresa. "Do you really think Jock would come after the shelter?"

Her green eyes brimmed with tears as she nodded. "He threatened to ruin everything I loved. This place is at the top of the list for me. Besides," she sniffed, "he hates you, Lily. For some reason, he counts you as one of the reasons I left him."

"And why would he do that?"

She shrugged. "Because you are. Before I met you, I'm not sure I would have had the strength to do it. The idea of upending my life and starting over petrified me. But you did it, and you're so happy now. It made me believe I could do the same." Her voice caught, and she took a deep breath before continuing, "I told him as much the night I left, when he said I would never make it without him. He'd gotten so angry when I mentioned you." She sat down in a nearby chair, her shoulders slumping as she stared at the floor. "I'm so sorry, Lily. I'm sorry my messy life is spilling over onto the rescue.

I went to her and squeezed her shoulder. "We don't know for sure this is Jock's doing." There was a small faction in Moonrise who was not crazy about having pit bulls in town. Any one of those jerks could have called in a complaint. Besides, even if it was Jock, Theresa wasn't responsible for his bad behavior, and it wouldn't change our circumstances to blame her. "Why don't you call the number on the notice and find out what's going on, and I'll go wake up Parker."

Keep reading! Get Pit and Miss Murder at your favorite store!

PARANORMAL MYSTERIES & ROMANCES
BY RENEE GEORGE

Witchin' Impossible Paranormal Mysteries

Witchin' Impossible (Book 1)

Rogue Coven (Book 2)

Familiar Protocol (Booke 3)

Mr & Mrs. Shift (Book 4)

FurOut (Book 5)

Barkside of the Moon Paranormal Mysteries

Pit Perfect Murder (Book 1)

Murder & The Money Pit (Book 2)

The Pit List Murders (Book 3)

Pit & Miss Murder (Book 4)

The Prune Pit Murder (Book 5)

Two Pits and A Little Murder (Book 6)

Pits and Pieces of Murder (Book 7)

Pittie Party Murder (Book 8)

Peculiar Mysteries & Romances

You've Got Tail (Book 1)

My Furry Valentine (Book 2)

Thank You For Not Shifting (Book 3)

My Hairy Halloween (Book 4)

In the Midnight Howl (Book 5)

Furred Lines (Book 6)

My Wolfy Wedding (Book 7)

Who Let The Wolves Out? (Book 8)

My Thanksgiving Faux Paw (Book 9)

Grimoires of a Middle-aged Witch

Earth Spells Are Easy (Book 1)

Spell On Fire (Book 2)

When the Spells Blows (Book 3)

Spell Over Troubled Water (Book 4)

Ghost in the Spell (Book 5)

Destiny of a Middle-aged Witch

Burning Djinn of Fire (Book 1)

Djinn Bottle Blues (Book 2)

Stand By Your Djinn (Book 3)

Nora Black Midlife Psychic Mysteries

Sense & Scent Ability (Book 1)

For Whom the Smell Tolls (Book 2)

War of the Noses (Book 3)

Aroma With A View (Book 4)

Spice and Prejudice (Book 5)

Age of Inno-Scents (Book 6)

Aroma Holiday (Book 7)

Vapes of Wrath (Book 8)

The Scented Cipher (Book 9)

Of Spice and Men (Book 10)

Hex Drive

Hex Me, Baby, One More Time (Book 1)

Oops, I Hexed It Again (Book 2)

I Want Your Hex (Book 3)

Hex Me With Your Best Shot (Book 4)

Hex Me All Night Long (Book 5)

ABOUT THE AUTHOR

USA Today Bestselling Author, Renee George writes paranormal mysteries and romances because she loves all things whodunit, Other-worldly, and weird. Also, she wishes her pittie, the adorable Kona, could talk. Or at least be more like Scooby-Doo and help her unmask villains at the haunted house up the street.

When she's not writing about mystery-solving werecougars or the adventures of a hapless psychic living among shapeshifters, she dons her super-hero cape and rescues kittens. Okay, the kitten totally showed up one day and suddenly she's got a new pet named Simon.

She lives in Missouri with her family and spends her non-writing time doing really cool stuff...like watching TV and cleaning up dog poop.

Join My Newsletter

Follow Me On Bookbub!

Join Renee's Rebel Readers on Facebook!